Blue Skies

Blue Skies

Karin Craft

CONTENTS

CONTENTS

This book is dedicated to my brother, Andrew. He has been huge part of my life and a joy to have as a sibling. He has taught me so much. I love you, Andrew!

I also dedicate this book to my sister, Elena. She has been a wonderful encouragement to me and a great editor!

How many of us want to be noticed? I mean *really* noticed. I suppose there are a few who like to be in the limelight. That's not me. I'd much rather sit in the back and just watch and observe rather than participate. Yes, I'm the type of person who will sit in a Starbucks, stare at her cup, and listen to all the conversations around me.

I say this, but then as I sit in the back of my classroom, I still half-hope someone will turn around and notice me all the same. Does that make sense? I guess not, but I'm a teenager. I think I'm not supposed to make sense.

I'm staring at my notebook as my teacher is talking-- something about bank statements. It's my last class of the day and I'm already planning the rest of my day. I work today, then home for one of our pizza nights. I think I feel like supreme tonight. I'll just pick off the mushrooms for Andrew; I'm sure he won't mind.

I sigh and glance at my watch. Fifteen minutes to go. I start softly tapping my pencil on my notebook. So bored.

The guy sitting next to me, nudges me. I glance at him and quickly stop the tapping. "Sorry," I whisper.

Jeremy just smiles and says, "I'm bored too."

No surprise there. We're three months into the class and every day it's the same story. Oh well. I signed up for this class because I knew it'd be easy, but it has been *brutal* to stay awake. Plus, I have had a half-crush on Jeremy for a few months and sitting next to him in this class hasn't helped the crush go away. I know he's out of my league anyway.

Last week, he asked my opinion about asking someone to the prom. For a few minutes, I thought he was leading up to asking me. I was thinking about what I would say if he asked--half hoping he would and then also hoping he wouldn't. Come to find out, he was planning to ask my best friend, Amber. He figured I'd be a good source to get information to ask her, I suppose. Since then, it's been even more awkward--at least for me.

At last, the bell rings and all of us jump up to file out the door. Poor Mr. Whitley has to move out of our way so we won't step on his toes. I try to smile at him as I pass by and nod goodbye to him.

I start heading out to my bike and Jeremy isn't far behind. I figure I should stop and walk with him.

"So, have you asked Amber?" I ask. Might as well get it out there in the open and pretend it doesn't matter. I mean, I can't even say I'm jealous--not about Jeremy anyway. If I'm completely honest with myself, there are times I might be jealous of Amber. She is so vivacious and beautiful. I feel so boring next to her; my brown hair to her blonde, my short stature to her tall, graceful one. You meet Amber Ramsey and you want to be her friend, you meet me and you think "Who was that again?" Amber and I met when we were in kindergarten and we have been best friends ever since. It doesn't hurt that we both live in the same housing development and our houses arc about a 10 minute walk apart, also. Honestly, I'd say I have few friends. I just don't make friends easily.

"Not yet." Jeremy admitted. "I think I'll ask her tomorrow at lunch. Do you know if anyone else has asked her?"

"I don't think so." I say as I get my bike unlocked. I settle my backpack on both shoulders and get on my bike. "Well, see ya."

"Yeah see you in Finance tomorrow."

"Oh yay" I don't have far to go from school to my work, which is good because today it seems to be rather overcast. April showers, right? Well, at least it's not raining at the moment.

As I arrive at the entrance of the library, I chain up my bike in its usual spot and head through the doors. I work at the library every day for a couple of hours. My mother thought it would be a great idea since I love to read. What better place for me to work than surrounded by books? I suppose if my job was reading the books it'd be perfect. But no, my job is *shelving* the books. I really shouldn't complain. It's a decent job and I like my boss.

Silas Hutchinson isn't the typical librarian, though he does wear glasses. He is outgoing and kind to everyone who comes into the library. Yet, he still has a very nerd-y vibe to him. That's ok, because I know I do too!

Silas smiles at me as I come in and asks how I was doing. I state that I am fine and roll the cart to the shelves to start reshelving. There's something about a job that is mind-numbing. I can think of a million things while checking Dewey decimals. I am thinking about what movie to watch with Andrew tonight. We typically watch movies together when it's pizza night and he definitely likes animated films. He lets us know by squealing in excitement or rocking his wheelchair back and forth. We've noticed he tends to get more excited about movies with singing, as well. I am going through our usual movies in my mind but I feel like watching something different. I think I'll check out Netflix or Disney+ once I order the pizza.

Every Thursday night my parents have a date night, and I need to watch my brother, Andrew. Sometimes Amber comes over and hangs out with us, but I think she's watching her two youngest siblings tonight, too. She's the oldest of four; I just have one brother.

My brother, Andrew, is 5 years younger than I and he has cerebral palsy. He is severely handicapped. He is in a wheelchair and is non verbal. Despite this, he communicates with us. Talk about not wanting to be noticed. We go to the store, we get stares. We go to church, we get stares. We go to a restaurant, we get stares. Am I embarrassed of my brother? No, I'm not but I certainly don't like being the center of attention, either. In today's day and age, I rarely hear people make fun of Andrew. I know that wouldn't have been the case even fifteen years ago. However, instead of not making fun, people avoid him. Or sometimes they avoid our family.

We sit in a pew at church and another family will sit at the opposite end of it. Or at the end of the service, people will come up to talk to my parents or me but won't acknowledge him there. It's nothing overt but the daily, or weekly occurrence, makes it so noticeable.

I look down and notice that my cart is empty. I roll it over and get the other cart by the circulation desk. I resume my work.

I'm not saying I expect perfect strangers to come up to our family and strike up a conversation with my parents and Andrew. I wouldn't want that. However, it'd be nice if someone comes to talk to me and they acknowledge Andrew's existence. I can count on one hand the people in my life who do that--aside from my family. Want the list? Our next door neighbor, Rosa; my mom's friend from work, Sara; and Amber. That's it.

I continue my work. I'm nearly finished with the second cart. I look at the clock on the back wall and figure that this would be the perfect time to be done.

I wheel the empty cart back over to Silas. I grab my backpack from behind the desk where I deposited it and say goodbye to Silas. He waves goodbye to me and I head out.

It is still overcast and not raining. I'm glad. I hate biking in the rain. My mom--and Amber--have pressured me to get my driver's license. I don't know why but I have no desire to get behind the wheel. So many things could go wrong. I much prefer to have others have that stress so I never have to deal with it. If it's pouring down, I've called Amber to pick me up. Typically she has something to do after school, and this time of year, it's soccer.

I bike the familiar route home and I'm glad for the wind in my face. It feels so refreshing. The ride usually takes 10 to 15 minutes, so it's not long until I arrive at our gate. You know the house you see on the street and you sort of cringe and think, "What the heck are the owners thinking putting such bright colors on that house?" Yeah, I live in that house.

For some reason, my parents decided to paint the house a bright blue with a red door. They certainly didn't ask six year old me when they got it in their heads.

As I get off my bike, I wave a hello to Rosa as she is outside watering her garden. Rosa is a retired teacher, and lives by herself. Usually she has on bright clothes and today she didn't disappoint. Today's outfit is a compilation of neon yellow and pink. She waves back, "Hello, Rita! How was your day?"

"It was good, Ms. Rosa. Yours?"

"Same old, Same old. But at my age, I guess you can't complain, eh?"

I laugh as I enter our front door. Once inside, I see Andrew in our family room. I go and give him a hug. Mom is running back and forth making sure she has everything ready for Andrew and me. She says, "I've put all of Andrew's medicine on the counter and his pj's on his bed."

"I know, Mom. You do that *every* time you leave." Mom gives me her half smile. I suppose I should've said that in a kinder way. Andrew care takes its toll on my parents. You don't realize how much work it can be taking care of a disabled son--it's not just the day-to-day care (which is enough as it is), it's the numerous doctors' appointments, the meetings at school. The list can go on and on. And they have the care for the rest of Andrew's life. It never goes away.

"Mom, don't worry about it. I remember where everything is. Have fun tonight and enjoy yourself," I say in apology.

"Yes, I know. And you can call me if you can't find something for Andrew."

"Yes."

Dad just came in, then. "Ready to go, hon?"

"Yes, just need to grab my purse and put on shoes, then I'll be good to go!" Mom says as she heads to their bedroom.

"Where are you guys going tonight, Dad?"

"I'm not sure. I figured we'd pick in the car. Any ideas?"

"You know me. I always love pizza!"

"Oh yeah, that reminds me. Here's the $20 for your pizza!" He hands me a twenty dollar bill and then when Mom returns with purse in hand, they leave.

I kiss Andrew's head and ask him, "What do you think about supreme tonight? I know you don't like mushrooms, but you like everything else!"

Andrew does his classic smile and his little dance in his wheelchair. Whenever he's excited he moves around in his wheelchair. When he's *really* excited, he squeals. I grab his hand as he is waving his arm around. "I know, I'm excited about having pizza, too!"

I open the Domino's app and place my order . Then, I turn on the TV and click on Netflix. Nothing catches my eye. I click the home button and select Disney+. I browse the movies. Andrew likes animation, the bright colors capture his attention.

"What about *Moana*, Andrew? I think it's been a long

time since we have seen it! It used to be my favorite movie, before you were even born! I bet you would like the music, too." I click on that and start the movie. I kiss him on his forehead as I head to the kitchen to prepare his medicine. He should have his medicine 30 minutes before eating so I gather up his pills that Mom placed on the counter. I get a glass of water and bring it back to Andrew. I place one pill at a time on his tongue and let him take a drink. After all the pills are taken, I massage his throat to make sure it goes down smoothly. Andrew looks at me and smiles again. "Oh, I know, Andrew. I love you, too." I pull my chair next to his wheelchair and we watch *Moana* together.

When the knock on the door finally happens, I am ready for dinner! I grab the twenty and go to the door. It's the usual delivery guy, Mike. "Hi, Mike."

"Supreme this time, huh?"

"Yeah, figured I'd switch it up now and then."

I hand him the money and he gives me the change, with the pizza. "Thanks," I say as I give him his tip.

"Ok, bye. See you next week!"

"Alright." I shut the door and grab the paper plates in the kitchen. Bringing the pizza and the plates into the family room, I lay them both on the coffee table. I put a piece on a plate and meticulously take off mushrooms. "See? I told you I'd take them off for you." Grabbing a knife and fork, I start cutting up the pizza in bite size pieces. I grab his bib hanging up in the kitchen and put it on him. I give him a piece of the cut pizza . While he's chewing, I get myself a slice.

With his pizza gone, Andrew starts dancing in his chair. "Mmmm, mmmm" as he moves around.

"You want more? Ok, ok, hold on a second. Let me get one ready." I prepare another piece for Andrew and resume feeding him.

After his two slices, I get up and clean up Andrew. I put his plastic bib in the trash and grab a washcloth from the sink. I wipe off Andrew's face and hands from pizza sauce and cheese.

"Ok, you want to finish up the movie, Andrew? Or just head to bed?"

Andrew shakes his head side to side, "Mmmmhmmm" and gives me another smile.

"Well how about a few more minutes, I think the movie is almost over. Then, I need to get you ready for bed. Don't tell Mom that I let you stay up!"

I hold Andrew's hand and stroke the back of it, just the way he likes it. He smiles again and giggles. I smile back at him.

The movie ends and I get up from my seat. I wheel Andrew to his bedroom, talking to him as I go. After the bedtime routine is complete (changing brief, brushing teeth, washing face, changing clothes), I grab Andrew around his waist and heft him from the wheelchair to the bed. I cover him with his bedding, and kiss him goodnight. I stroke his dirty blonde hair as he closes his eyes. When they are closed, I stand up and head to the door.

"I love you, Andrew. Good night." I say then turn off the light and shut the door.

I go to my room and I glance around for my cat. He usually is curled up on my bed, but he's not there now. I'm not exactly a neat person, I'll be the first to admit. There are clothes scattered about the room, books piled in random stacks on my desk, headboard, and floor. Just then, Elgato, my cat, comes out of my closet. He rubs against my leg and I pick him up. "*Hola, Elgato. Te amo, tambien.*"

I stroke the fur of my cat. He has brown and black stripes with some white patches thrown in. He's two years old, a birthday present for my sixteenth birthday. I have taken Spanish every year of high school. I don't pretend to be fluent but I thought I'd name him Elgato to be funny (*El gato* means "the cat".) Then, I started to practice my Spanish on him and that turned to me *only* speaking Spanish to him.

"*Soy cansada. Y tu?*" Elgato starts purring in response and I giggle. I sigh and figure I should retrieve my backpack and start the history homework. A few minutes later, I hear the front door open and my parents' voices. Mom peeks in and asks, "How'd everything go?"

"Fine, Mom. We had fun. Andrew had two pieces of pizza, tonight. I think I'm training him to like pizza *almost* as much as I do!"

She laughs and comes into the room to give me a hug. "Thanks for watching him; it's nice to be able to have time with your father."

I hug her back and said, "You deserve it, Mom."

After saying our good nights, she heads to their room. I resume my homework but it's hard to concentrate. My phone rings just then and it's Amber.

"Hi, Amber!"

"Hey yourself. Whatcha up to?"

"Oh, finishing up homework. You?"

"Nothing much. Got Sarah to bed on time, surprise! But Elias wasn't so easy." Those are her two youngest siblings. Sarah is 4 and Elias 6; they can be quite a handful.

"Good job! Andrew and I had fun watching *Moana* tonight."

"So you fill out college applications, yet?" This has been an almost daily question by Amber. I want to go to college, I do. But I'm not sure I want to go *now*. I don't know what I want to be when I grow up!

"Ugh. No, and I haven't gotten my license, and I'm going to stay in my parent's house until I'm thirty. Those are my plans!"

Amber laughs and switches topics. "Guess what I've started doing?"

"I don't know. What?"

"I'm going to run a marathon! I started training for it."

"You're insane, you know that, right? *Insane!*"

"Yeah, and the only time I really have to run is in the morning, so I need to get up early to do that. Mom is making me take Duke along with me. He is *so* out of shape!" Duke is her dog and I *really* don't like dogs. They are either too small and yippy and annoying or too big and can bite off my arm or something.

"Just don't run over here with him! I don't want to wake up with Duke and you staring at me while I sleep!"

"Oh, we already do that. It's fun to watch you snore."

I laugh. "That's so creepy."

"Well 5 am is going to come way too soon, I should probably go. See you in Spanish?"

"Yep. Good night!"

"Night."

Spanish class is the only class that Amber and I have together. I have English, Spanish, history, creative writing, one study hall, and the rest of my classes are joke classes (including the Finance class with Jeremy). It's my senior year, I think it should be fun. Amber, on the other hand, has a ton of AP classes, and she's working non stop on homework. I have no idea how she does all that she does. She is the most ambitious person I know. She has a 5 year plan and is sticking to it. She'll be going to University of Maryland next year and will be doing their pre-med program. Me? No idea where I'll go and what I want to do. I figure I'll graduate first, then decide.

I yawn and look at my homework. Eh, I'll just finish it in study hall. It's right before history anyway. I figure I'll read a bit before falling asleep. Once I'm settled in bed, Elgato comes to his usual spot and curls up by head. *Buenas noches, Elgato.*

The alarm from my phone wakes me up. I stayed up *way* too late reading. I had to finish my book and just couldn't put it down! I roll over and pull the pillow over my head. Elgato meows in protest. *Lo siento,* I mumble to him and close my eyes...just for a minute.

My mom bursts in. "Rita, you're not up yet? Get up. You have 15 minutes before you need to leave for school!"

I bolt upright and look at the time. Crap! I slept another 30 minutes. I quickly brush my teeth while trying to get dressed. A truly heroic effort!

I rush out the door, stuffing a pop tart in my mouth, two minutes late. I'll try to bike fast to make up the time. My favorite class is creative writing and it's my first class. Currently, the teacher is having us describe ourselves as a color. It's due on Monday and I still haven't settled on a color. How do you define yourself as a color? I don't even know. Maybe I'll ask Amber.

I rush into my class just as the bell goes off. Ms. Perkins looks up from her desk as I run into the classroom. She smiles at me in greeting while I settle into my seat.

And so another day begins.

The day passes uneventfully without any major catastrophes and I find myself on my bike again heading home from work. I am tired but glad it's Friday. I actually have no plans this weekend, and I'm hoping Amber's free, too. Maybe we can go see a movie or something.

As I turn into Pine Crest, our housing development, I hear my phone ring. I just let it go to voicemail as I'm almost home.

After getting off my bike, and chaining in its usual spot in the backyard, I head into our house. I see Andrew through the sliding glass door in the kitchen with Dad. When Dad's cooking dinner on Fridays, he brings Andrew in. I think Andrew likes the smell of the cooking and I think Dad likes the company. He talks to Andrew while he's making dinner. It's a win/win situation, I suppose. I peek in and say hi and then head to my room. This time Elgato is at his usual spot on my bed.

I sit roughly on the bed just to make the bed bounce and jostle Elgato. He opens up one eye, then the other, and I swear he glares at me. I laugh and pet him. I grab the phone from my backpack and saw it was Amber who called. I quickly hit her number to call her back.

She answers after the first ring. "Hi, I saw you called. What's up?"

She sniffs and asks, "Wanna meet me at the lake?"

She is referring to the lake that is in our housing development and it is actually between our houses. I can tell she has been crying from the tremor in her voice, so I quickly agree. I go back to the kitchen and let my parents know I am heading to the lake. I give Andrew a kiss on his cheek and squeeze his hand goodbye.

I head to our normal spot, a picnic table by the lake. I arrive before Amber and I lean against the tree next to the table. I close my eyes and take a deep breath. Spring is definitely in the air. I remember climbing the tree and pretending it was a castle with Amber. We were princesses in need of rescuing. Once, maybe when we were eight, I got stuck in the tree and *really* needed to be rescued. Amber had to run home to get her father to get me out. I smile at the memory.

I glance towards Amber's home and see her walking towards me. Her blonde hair glistens in the sun. How can she so effortlessly be beautiful? "Remember when I got stuck in the tree?" I ask when Amber is close enough to hear. She nods her head.

"What's wrong?" I ask as soon as I notice her red eyes.

"Mom and Dad are fighting again. Mom took Sarah and Elias to Grandma's house. Dad just slammed his door to the office after they left, and I haven't seen him since. Jenny at least didn't see it; she is at Allison's house tonight. I'm not sure what's going to happen, but it was the worst I've heard them fight, Rita."

"I thought the counseling was going well for them."

"Yeah, me too."

Amber sits on the bench and sighs. "Times like these, I can't wait to go to college just to get out of the house. But what about Sarah, Elias and Jenny? I can't leave them alone with Mom and Dad. Not when they fight like that! It was awful."

I sit down next to her and hug her. I wish I could say something to make her magically feel better. I stare at the ground and see something shiny in the dirt. I bend down and pick it up. It's a normal, small rock, but it had both silver and blue-green flecks in it. I smile and say, "Remember how we used to collect rocks?"

"Yeah I still have my rock collection, believe it or not. It's still in that shoebox under my bed."

I hand her the rock I picked up. "Add that to your collection." She fiddles with the rock for a few moments.

"One thing I've learned living with Andrew, you can't always fix the problem. It's how you react to those un-fixable problems that define you. You can't fix your parents' marriage, you have no control over their relationship, and nor should you. You can only be in charge of *you*. Be the best big sister to your siblings. You can help around the house, I guess. Do little things to make your parents' lives easier. I don't know, you probably can come up with better ideas than I can. But I guess you know what I mean."

Amber sniffs, staring at the rock in her hands. "Yeah, I guess. I wish I could do more, though."

We sit there in quiet for a few minutes. "Did you get up and run this morning?" I ask, to get her thinking about something else, maybe.

"Yeah. I had to drag Duke along. After the first mile, I guess he got tired and I had to run with my hand outstretched behind me. One of these days, maybe he'll get in shape and can actually keep up with me!"

I laugh a little. "I bet that was kinda funny to watch."

"I suppose. Just was annoying!"

"You know you can come over anytime and bring your siblings--if you need. I know Sarah still cries when she sees Andrew, but I think she'll get used to him, eventually."

"Yeah I wish she wasn't so scared of him."

"It just takes time. Eventually she'll want to sit on his lap and ride around on his wheelchair, I'm sure."

Amber giggles. "I guess you're right." She gives me a quick hug. "Thanks, Rita. I love you."

"Awww. I love you, too. I wish I could do more!" I pause. I take a breath and ask, "Hey, I have a project in my writing class. I'm supposed to describe myself as a color. Any ideas? I'm drawing a blank, and it's due on Monday."

Amber pauses to think. "You know, I'll have to get back with you. I'll think on it and let you know later, alright?"

"Ok, thanks" I agree. I shrug my shoulders, "I couldn't come up with a color, and I've been thinking of it all week. So good luck with that!"

Amber chuckles. "Well, I'll let you know." She stops and hits her forehead with the palm of her hand. "Wow. I completely forgot to tell you. Guess who asked me to the prom today?"

I tap my chin with my finger. "Hmmm...could it possibly be Jeremy?"

She punches me in the shoulder. "How'd you know?"

"He asked me in Finance last week if you were going with anyone else. I told him, 'What, Amber? Pfft, she's got a list mile long but can't decide who to go with.' I guess he decided to throw his hat in the ring."

Amber rolls her eyes. "You're crazy."

"So, what did you say?"

"I said sure."

"Well I guess I should head back." Amber says looking at the time. "I have some homework I need to get started on. I won't have to get up as early tomorrow morning, at least."

"Ok. Do you want to do something tomorrow afternoon? I was thinking maybe a movie. Maybe we can take our siblings."

"Yeah let's do that. I'll check out what movies are out and text you." Amber stands up and gives me a quick hug. She shows me the rock, still in hand. "Thanks for this. I'll put it with the others. Do you still have your rock collection?"

I laugh. "I am sure I still have it somewhere. Maybe in the back of my closet?" I shrug my shoulders. Amber laughs because she knows the extent of my organizational skills.

Amber heads to the direction of her house; she turns around to give me one final wave goodbye. I wave back and head toward home. I love spring and it has definitely arrived. I didn't really take the time to notice on the way to the lake earlier, but I admire the blooming flowers and listen to the birds chirping as I walk back to my house. My grandma can name every flower she walks by. I envy that now! Too bad she lives in another state. Otherwise, I'd bug her to teach me!

I stop walking for a minute and close my eyes. I feel the warmth of the spring sun on my head and I lift up my face to it. I can't help it. I stretch out my arms and slowly spin in a circle. I'm sad my friend is going through a hard time, but for the moment I'm happy. I love spring!

After arriving home, I could tell that my parents and Andrew started dinner without me. I come to the kitchen and grab myself a plate and sit down with them. I start to eat.

Dad was feeding Andrew tonight and Andrew's enjoying it. When I sit down, Andrew smiles at me and then grabs Dad's hand for another piece. "Ok, ok, son. Just be patient!" Dad says as he gives him another bite.

"Hey Mom and Dad. Amber and I were talking just now. We are thinking of maybe taking Andrew and her brother and sisters to the movies tomorrow afternoon. That okay?"

"Sure, honey. I don't think we have any plans then," states Mom.

I turn to Andrew. "How about you? Want to go?" Andrew just giggles; he loves the attention. "It's a date, then!"

When dinner's over, I help Mom clear up the dishes while Dad cleans up Andrew. When he's finished, Dad wheels Andrew to the bathroom to give him a shower and get him ready for bed.

"How was school today?" Mom chats as we do the dishes. I stand next to her ready to dry the dishes as she hands them to me.

"Ok I guess. Nothing really to report. I just have one writing assignment to do this weekend, so not too much homework."

"I can't believe you're almost done with high school! My baby's growing up!" Mom says as she pinches my cheek with a soapy finger. I roll my eyes as I grab the last dish from her other hand. Once it's put away in the cupboard, I hang up the dish towel and head to my room.

As I pass by the bathroom, I hear Dad finishing up Andrew's shower. I knock on the door and ask if Dad needs any help. With a "No, thank you" through the door, I continue on to my bedroom for the night.

3 |

All of us dash through the doors of the movie theater (Jenny holding the door for Andrew and me) to get out of the pouring rain. Andrew squeals in delight; I guess he had a lot of fun with the mad sprint from the van to the movie theater in the wheelchair. To be honest, I think I would've enjoyed the ride if it were me.

As we wait in line, all 6 of us, I thank Amber for driving us. She had to drive our wheelchair van because of Andrew. She shrugs her shoulders. "Eh, it's no big deal. I just hate parking the beast. Sorry we had a longer run than necessary." I look at Andrew and myself. We have water everywhere and are soaking wet, something akin to drowned cats. I look at the Ramseys. Somehow, despite dashing in the rain *all* of them looked like they just stepped out of a salon or something. How do they do that?

"It's alright, I think we made Andrew's day with that run."

Amber smiles and gives Andrew a hug, "Was that fun?" Andrew smiles in return.

I notice Sarah standing on other side of Amber and eying Andrew nervously. She is holding Jenny's hand while we are waiting in line. I ask Sarah, "Do you want a ride on Andrew's wheelchair?"

Sarah just shakes her head quietly and edges closer to Jenny. Oh well, it was worth a try. Like I said to Amber yesterday, it'll take time but she'll eventually get used to Andrew.

I can feel the stares start on my back; people turning to look as they walk by. You'd think I'd be used to it by now, but sometimes it is hard to ignore. I start to blush which makes it even worse. I'm not embarrassed by Andrew, but I wish that sometimes we weren't so conspicuous! Once we got our tickets (from a guy that wouldn't meet our eyes--another usual occurrence) and our popcorn, we head to our theater. I brake Andrew's wheelchair in the handicapped spot and we all file in around his spot. I sit down next to Andrew and Amber settles in next to me. As Amber is handing out the popcorn to her sisters and brother, she announces, "I've come up with a color for you, by the way."

"Oh yeah? What's that?"

"Sky blue."

I laugh. "Is that an allusion to my house?" She groans. She likes the color of my house, almost as much as I do.

"No. But I guess with your house in mind, I'll change it to *light* sky blue."

"Heh, okay. Why that color?"

"Well, sometimes you will go days without noticing the sky. Then, you get days like today and the absence of it makes you miss it. Or just some days you happen to notice the sky and when you do, it's all you can see."

I am speechless. Thankfully I don't need to come up with

a rejoinder as the previews just then start. We settle into all our seats and start to watch the movie. As the lights dim, Andrew starts dancing in his chair and flinging his arm around. He squeals once. I grab his hand and stroke it. "Shhh" I whisper to him. "We have to be quiet."

He calms down. "Mmmmmmm," he says.

We all file out of the door, with the credits and music still playing. Sarah is excitedly telling Elias her favorite part of the movie.

"And *then*, the dog saves the girl. The girl names him 'Fivo'."

Elias impatiently tells her, "I know. I just saw the movie, too, remember?"

Amber jumps in to quiet the argument that would be soon to follow. "I think that was my favorite part, too, Sarah." She turns to look sternly at Elias and Elias shrugs his shoulders in embarrassment.

While Amber and the younger girls go to the restroom, I stand outside with Andrew and Elias. I glance through the doors and notice that it's no longer pouring. I think maybe it's just drizzling now. Regardless, we'll not need to run to the van.

Once everyone is ready we head out the door and into the rain. I try to keep Andrew's head dry with his hood, but it won't stay on. Oh well. At least the rain is a warm rain. Everyone files into the van, and I hand the remote for the lift to Elias. Elias likes to control the lift while I stand with Andrew and his wheelchair in the lift.

A few minutes later, we are all buckled in our respective seats and Amber pulls out of our parking spot.

Later that night, I sit down at my desk and and open up my laptop. I am grateful for Amber's suggestion and have been ruminating on it since Andrew and I came home.

I stare at my laptop screen for several minutes, not sure how to start. I shrug my shoulders and figure that I'll just start and see how it goes.

I am a color that blends in the background, a color that you don't normally detect. When you look at the sky or perhaps when you see some flowers blooming, you'll see me. You won't necessarily notice me but you'll see me.

I sigh and sit back in my chair, closing my eyes. I try to picture what I'm going to write next. Blending in the background, that's me. I don't like to make waves or be noticed, and sometimes (like this afternoon) it can't be avoided. I wish I could brush off the stares and the looks but I can't. I wish I could do more, I wish I could have the courage to turn and look at the people and say, "Something wrong?" I laugh. That's so not me, but I wish I could. Elgato jumps up and starts walking on my desk, and he makes the short circuit around it. Before too long, he starts walking on my laptop, purring, trying to get me to pet him. My eyes pop open and command him. *Bajate!* Elgato pounces to the floor. Quickly I delete all his extraneous typing and then I pick him up and put him on my lap. I guess I've not paid that much attention to him today. I start petting him and he resumes purring.

My thoughts are interrupted when I get a text. I had sent

Amber a text earlier asking her how things were with her parents because I was unable to ask her while we were at the movies. That's not a type of question you ask with listening ears nearby.

I look at the text and see it is from Amber. "Ok I guess. Mom and Dad are not talking. Rest of us are walking on eggshells."

"Too late to call?" Amber shares a room with her sisters and I figured she probably was getting ready for bed.

"Yes," is the response.

We text back and forth for several minutes. Come to find out, Amber's mom said that she'd like to take Amber out sometime in the next week. Amber assumes it'll be to discuss the future and how it'd look like next year. Amber is dreading that conversation, and I don't blame her.

Once our texting conversation is done, I reread what I started on the laptop. I resume my effort; I'd really like to finish this and be done with work tonight. Elgato is asleep on my lap and I scoot my chair closer to the laptop, trying not to wake him. I definitely don't want him walking on my laptop again!

For some reason, I always do my best work when everyone's asleep. Something about it being so quiet or peaceful. Regardless, my block is gone and I type furiously. I think this might be my best work, yet.

4

I'm holding Andrew's hand as we wait for our parents to finish talking to people. I've pointed Andrew's chair at a diagonal so that we both can look out the glass doors. At the moment I'm watching some birds hopping around in the grass. Along with flowers, my grandma can identify birds. I know nothing about birds, but there is something relaxing watching them.

People are milling around us. I looked for the Ramsey family as we were filing into church and didn't see them. Just as the service was about to start,though, they arrived and sat in the back. I had hoped to speak to them after, but the family was quick to leave. I caught Amber's eye before I got there and she just shrugged. She didn't seem her usual bubbly self. I am staring at the birds, thinking about Amber. Is there something I can do? Can I help? I don't even know. I want to talk to my parents, but something this personal, I feel like it's not my place to tell. What should I do?

"Hi," says someone right behind me. I jump as I turn around. It is David Gibson. He's a year younger than I and attends another high school. He is about 6 feet tall, and has dark hair. He has grown up in the church too. As with most people in the church, they don't avoid me when I'm with Andrew. But they don't acknowledge or greet Andrew either.

"Wow, Dave. You surprised me! I didn't even hear you."

"Yeah, sorry. What are you looking at anyway?"

I turn back to look out the glass door. "I dunno. I was just watching these birds. Nothing too exciting, really."

"Jeremy told me he asked Amber to the prom." David says, moving up to stand next to me. Dave and Jeremy were on the same soccer team at the Y when they were in elementary school and stayed friends. He looks out at the birds, too.

"Yeah. She said yes." I give him a sidelong glance. Why is he here? If he's going to strike up a conversation, it's usually with Amber right next to me. To be honest, very rarely at church do I not have Amber right by me.

"Do you have a date to the prom?" He asks me, still staring outside. I am shocked and turn to stare at him. I don't even know what to say in response. Andrew starts moving in his chair. He sees Mom and Dad approaching us. I don't want to not say anything to Dave. Am I jumping to conclusions? Did he just sort of ask me to my own prom?

"No, not yet," I say quickly before my parents arrive.

"Hi guys. Ready to go home?" Dad asks as he stands behind Andrew to wheel him to our van.

"Yeah sure. Bye, Dave. See you next week!"

Dave raises his hand goodbye and quickly walks away. I'm glad my parents came when they did so I wouldn't have to continue that awkward conversation--even more so with my racing thoughts. I'm sure I am overthinking what just happened. I wish Amber were here so I could ask her opinion on what happened.

I'll call her this afternoon, or maybe meet at the lake again. I quickly glance at the sky as we walk to the van and see that it's a muted blue, with some clouds. It is a gorgeous day.

I text Amber once we are in the van and heading home about meeting at the lake later today. Amber agrees and we set for 2 o'clock at our usual spot. I sigh and make a mental list of all the things I want to talk to her about.

We arrive home and I see Rosa in the yard gardening again. I haven't seen her in a few days, so I go over to her. This time she is wearing a bright blue and green outfit. "Hi Rosa!"

"Hi, yourself!"

I see her watering her plants and a light bulb goes off. "Hey, Rosa, do you think you could teach me about flowers? My grandma told me all the names of the flowers that we saw when we would hike, but I don't remember any of them. And it's been a while since we've visited her. I was at the lake the other day and I was thinking I wish I knew the flowers that I saw."

"Yes, that sounds wonderful. Maybe one day we can take Andrew and walk around the lake. I'm sure Andrew would like looking at the flowers too."

"Okay, sounds great! How about next Saturday afternoon? Hopefully it won't rain like it did yesterday!"

"Heh, yeah I imagine it won't be very pleasant for any of us if it's pouring down while we walk around the lake. But, sure, let's plan on this Saturday. I'll scrounge around for some of my flower books so we can look it up if I don't know. I'm looking forward to it!"

"Yeah me too. Thanks, Rosa. See you later!"

"Bye, Rita."

I turn around and take the ramp up to our front door. I guess my parents already brought Andrew into the house.

Dad is getting Andrew's medicine ready while Mom bustles around getting lunch prepared. Sunday lunch usually is a pretty lowkey meal--crackers and soup or sandwiches. I glance at my phone and I have about an hour before meeting Amber. I go to the kitchen and help Mom get things out for the meal.

At just before two, I start heading to the lake. I'm enjoying the sun on my back. There's something so rejuvenating about a spring day. In Maryland summers are so stifling; it's so humid. However, spring? Spring is so wonderful. I love it! I admit there is a bit of a bounce to my step as I head to the picnic table.

This time, Amber is waiting for me. She has her back turned to me, so she can't see me. She is sitting on the bench, cupping her head in her hands. She is looking at the water. The sun is bouncing off her blonde curls. Once again, I think to myself how I wish I were more like her. I know she has her flaws, as does everyone--but I sometimes wish I had been given a smidgen of her personality, just enough to be more assertive and sure of myself.

I walk up closer and she hears me and turns around. She flashes me a quick smile and pats the spot next to her. I sit down next to her and look out onto the lake. "So you guys left rather quickly after the service."

Amber returns to her previous position. "Yeah, Mom didn't want to stay. Things are really tense, Rita. I'm actually kind of nervous. Mom wants to have us go out Thursday night. So, that's 2 weeks I'm gonna miss pizza night with you and Andrew! I'm so sorry."

"It's no problem." I give an exaggerated sigh. "Somehow we'll make it through and manage without you."

"I don't think so. You're hopeless, Rita. Speaking of, applied to any colleges yet?" She glances at me with a little smile.

I roll my eyes and and shake my head. I can tell she's trying for a sense of normalcy and I figure I'd oblige. "Remember? I'm staying at my parent's house til I'm 30 and I think I'm gonna get maybe 4 more cats. Elgato is getting lonely."

"What are you going to name them? Cat in 4 more languages? You should name one of those four "Cat" at least."

"Well then everyone will assume I named the cat 'Catherine.' Seems kind of pretentious don't you think?"

"Like I said, hopeless." She looks down and starts tracing some cracks in the picnic table wood.

"Anything I can do to help? I wish I could do something."

"Nah, I don't even know what I can do. As you said before, I have no control over Mom and Dad's relationship. I know that, but I still feel helpless. Like I need to do something. Jenny knows what's going on, but Elias and Sarah have no idea. They just can feel the tension and Mom and Dad have short tempers with their antics--well really short tempers with us all."

She pauses for a few minutes. I just stay there quietly, listening to the ducks and birds chirping in the trees. I told her it's how you approach an unfixable problem that defines you and that she's not in charge of her parents' relationship and I believe what I said. I truly do. But, if so, why do *I* feel that I'm responsible? If only I did the right thing, things would be better in the Ramsey household. I know that it is silly, but I must believe it at some level for me to feel this way. Am I a hypocrite?

Amber speaks up. "If I'm completely honest with myself, I think that's why I decided to start training for a marathon. I thought the counseling was going well, but I could still feel the tension. The training gets me out of the house more. Jenny is getting more involved in after-school things, too. She tried out for the play. Though, a seventh grade production of *A Midsummer Night's Dream* is probably not going to be all that spectacular. The two younger ones don't have ways to escape. I think that is why Sarah and Elias are acting out more than usual."

I have no words to say, really. I just nod my head silently.

Amber starts biting her fingernails; she does it when she's nervous and jittery. It's been a while since I've seen her this nervous. I think maybe the last time was when *she* was in the 7th grade play. After the performance she swore that she'd never again get on stage

I am trying to decide if I should tell her about my conversation with Dave. Should I bring it up to change the subject and get her mind off of her troubles, or should I just be quiet and listen, if she needs? I put my head in my hand, too and start drumming my fingers on my cheek. Suddenly, Amber sits up and decides for me. "Ok enough of this. Tell me something happy, something funny, I don't care! Just tell me something so I can think of something else!"

"Alrighty, then. I have a story to tell you!" I tell her what happened this morning with Dave.

She claps her hands excitedly and she starts making plans for the prom with the four of us. It's kind of funny that just a few days ago she wasn't even sure she wanted to go. I just let her be happy for the moment and make plans, nevermind that I'm not even sure Dave had asked me. I suppose I should clarify that with Dave. Ugh, not looking forward to that conversation.

I interrupt Amber's barrage of words. "So, do you think I can text Dave and ask him about the prom? I really don't want to talk to him in person about this!"

Ambers *tsks*. "Hold on a sec, let me call him."

"Ack! Not right now! I'm right here!"

"Shhhh. He won't need to know!" Amber giggles as she stands up.

I growl in frustration but quietly subside when I hear Dave pick up on the other end. "Hey, Dave! How are you doing?" She starts the conversation like a normal friendly conversation.

She nods her head. "Yeah, sorry about that. We had to head out of church pretty early."

For the next few minutes they talk about random things-- music, sports, and I think I even hear something about shoes. Then the topic of me comes up. I can tell because Amber starts looking at me with a smile. She isn't saying much on her end, just a "uh huh" and "oh really?" at apparently appropriate times. I think she's doing that on purpose so I can't tell what is being said!

After what seems like forever, Amber hangs up. She sits down next to me again. "So yeah we can continue planning prom stuff for the four of us."

"We? I only heard you planning!" I pause, then ask, "So, do I need to let him know yes or something?"

"Heh, yeah I think that might be a good idea."

"Crap. That means I need to bring up the conversation. Which brings me back to my original question...can I text him rather than *talk* to him?"

"I'd go with talk. But you need to wait until I can listen so I can quietly laugh at you while you stumble along--the both of you!"

"I'm not calling him now, if that's what you think!"

Amber laughs and agrees. It's good to see her laughing and I can't help but smile, too. We talk a few more minutes. Then, Amber gasps. "I have an idea. Let's have a pizza night at our house this week--you and Andrew can have an extra day of pizza! My parents are going to be gone Tuesday for counseling and I'm babysitting again. Bring Andrew over and you can call Dave then, too!"

"Sounds fun! Well not the calling part--that's ugh-worthy. I think I might develop laryngitis right about when that's supposed to happen. Everything else sounds fun, though! I'll ask Silas if I can leave early on Tuesday so we can start a movie earlier for Sarah and Elias."

Amber hugs me. "Thanks so much for once again being the best thing for me. I really don't know what I'd do without you."

I laugh. "Glad I could be of help, but really didn't do much."

Amber shakes her head. "You always put yourself down. I wish you wouldn't. You're by far the best person I know. I know you think you aren't noticed, but you're wrong. People notice you and appreciate the kindnesses you show them. Blue skies, Rita. Blue skies."

I nod my head, afraid to talk for fear of crying, and hug her back. Blue skies.

5

I pull into my driveway and take my bike around back. Mr. Silas graciously let me leave early like I had asked, even though there were 2 whole carts left to reshelve. I enter through the sliding door and let Mom know I am home. As soon as I came home from the lake Sunday afternoon, I let my parents know of our plans. So Mom is gathering up Andrew's medicine and getting him ready to leave.

I go over to Andrew and give him a hug, "Hey, buddy! You ready to go over to the Ramseys? We're going to have *so* much fun! We get pizza tonight. Yay!"

Andrew does his dance in excitement. Mom comes over and gives me the bag she put his medicine in. "I don't like you walking home in the dark. Text your dad when the movie's done and he will come pick you up in the van."

I sigh. "Alright, Mom. I'm sure it'll be just fine for us to walk home. I'm not going to push Andrew through the paths around the lake. We will be on sidewalks the whole time and all the streets are very well lit. But ok." The fastest path is through the middle, where the lake is. However, it is hard to push Andrew's wheelchair on non-paved paths. There is one leading to the path around the lake and another leading from the lake to where Amber's house is. The path leading to Amber's house is long and considerably very bumpy. Just walking on the sidewalk by the streets would add more time but wheelchair pushing will be much easier.

I go to the bedroom to leave my backpack and change clothes (I got a little sweaty on the ride home from school). I see Elgato on his spot and pat his head, *"Adios, mi amigo. Hasta luego!"*

In true form, he closes his eyes while glaring at me for rudely awakening him. He obviously is not sad to see me go!

I return to Mom and Andrew and I start pushing Andrew through the door. Mom held the front door open for me and we went down the ramp into our driveway. I wave at Mom and say, "I'll text Dad. Thank you!"

I start the walk, pushing Andrew. "It's been so long since I've walked to the Ramseys house, Andrew. And to be honest, I don't think I've ever *walked* this route. It's always been driving. I wonder how long it'll take to walk this. And I wonder how much my legs will be burning from it? I think Amber would be proud. Maybe I can train with her?" I laugh at my own joke. Andrew doesn't seem to care. He is dancing and excited to be outside in the warm sun.

"I know, I know! The sun feels great! I think you'll really enjoy our walk on Saturday. Will you help me learn the flowers we see?"

I realize I should probably text Amber to let her know we are on the way. As I do that, I'm talking to Andrew about our plans for the evening. *"And* Amber is *insisting* on me calling Dave, *while* she listens! I don't think I can do that. Will you run defense for me? Maybe wheel yourself between Amber and I? I don't know. I'm definitely not looking forward to this. I'm not even sure why I agreed to it. I mean, I guess it'll be good to have clarity and know for sure Dave meant to ask me to the prom, rather than third hand. But I don't know...."

I trail off as I start pushing up a pretty steep hill. Amber's street is at the top of the hill. Dang. I forgot about this hill. When we were kids, and it snowed, we would sled down this hill. And yep, it's still a big hill.

As I crest the hill, I'm sweating. I guess I shouldn't have even bothered changing.

"Yep," I say when I catch my breath, "I'm out of shape. I guess Amber will *not* have me training with her heh."

Thankfully, her house is the second one on the right once you turn on her street. So, we get to her front porch and I put Andrew's brakes on. I climb the 3 steps (using the railing for support, man, my legs are on fire!) and knock on the door. Duke immediately starts barking. Amber quickly opens the door, keeping Duke back with her legs, "Heyyy! So glad you guys came." She notices the sweat "Did you run here?"

"No! That hill! It's steep and hard to push Andrew up it. I had completely forgotten about it."

"Oh yeah, I always try to sprint up that hill at the end of my runs."

"Showoff!" I turn around, "Could you keep the door open and I'll get Andrew up these stairs?"

"Yeah sure, Let me get Duke outside so he won't run off and chase a squirrel or something. Be right back."

I go sit on the bottom step next to Andrew. "Yay! We made

it! I'm glad Dad's getting us tonight. I don't think I want to take you down that hill in the dark, well lit or not. Don't tell Mom that, though. It'll be our little secret! She can't know she is right; it'll go to her head."

Amber returns quickly. "Here, want me to get Andrew up the stairs and you hold the door?"

"No, it's alright. I can do it. Thank you." I unbrake his wheelchair and turn him around. We go up the 3 stairs backwards. As we wheel by her, me making sure to not run over her toes, Amber greets Andrew. "Hey Andrew! So glad you're here. We are going to have so much fun tonight. Plus, we may or may not embarrass your sister tonight...who knows?" We make it in the house and I continue going backwards until the small foyer opens up to the living room.

"I'm assuming this is where the pizza eating and the movie watching will be?"

"Yes! I haven't ordered the pizza yet. I was just about to do that when you got here. Let me do that, then I'll gather the kids and we can pick something. Any requests?"

"Nah, Andrew and I like animated movies and he likes the music. I guess I do too. But, really, whatever Elias and Sarah want."

"Thing is, there is *nothing* that they both will want. It's so frustrating heh. So I think I'll pick a movie and blame it on you two. Then they can't complain!"

"Sure, we will be the bad guys!" I agree as I maneuver Andrew's chair through the living room furniture. I get him next to the couch and I sit down on the edge of the couch next to him.

I grab his hand and start stroking it.

After a minute or two, Amber puts her phone down. "Ok! I am not going to pick a movie just yet. You have a phone call to make! I figure it'll be best before the festivities start and you won't find one excuse or another to not call." She leans over and pretends to whisper to Andrew behind her hand. "This is the part of the night I've planned to embarrass Rita, by the way. Be sure to watch her blush! Any bets on how long it'll take her? I say 30 seconds!"

"What! I thought I had more time to gather courage! My courage supply is *extremely* low right now! I think I expended it all coming up that stupid hill!" I laugh.

"No excuses and going up that hill didn't take courage, silly. Muscles, yes. Determination, yes. Courage, no."

"Semantics!" I laugh, but I'm inwardly running around in a circle screaming, "Ahhhhh!"

Amber looks at me and can tell. She grabs my hand. "It's ok, Rita. It's just Dave. What is the worst that can happen? You stumble over a few words? It's ok. He knows you. He knows you're quiet. Remember? He is quiet too."

I nod my head. "I know. But I *really* don't want to have this conversation. Maybe you and Jeremy should just go. I don't like the idea of a dance anyway. Do I need to go?"

"No. And if you don't want to, you shouldn't go. You do you. But, you also shouldn't be afraid to have hard conversations. Otherwise, you can't be real with people, you know? Does that make sense?"

I nod my head. "Yeah, it does. And you're right. I shouldn't be scared of this conversation. We've been friends with Dave for years. I'm just being ridiculous." I reach for my phone from my back pocket and bring it forward. "Ok. Let's do this."

I call Dave and put it on speaker so Amber can listen in. After a couple of rings, Dave picks up. "Hey Rita."

"Hi, um, Dave. This is Rita" Then I inwardly groan. *Of course it's Rita, and he knows because he already said "Hey, Rita". Great, we are off to a great start!* I look at Amber and she nods encouragingly.

"Yeah, um, so I'm sorry our conversation got cut short on Sunday..." I take a breath, "I wasn't sure if you were asking me to the prom or not. Were you?" I quickly say the last part just to get it out there. I can feel myself blushing. Grr, I hate that I do that.

Dave laughs. "Let me guess, Amber put you up to this. And, knowing Amber, she's right there listening. Hi Amber!"

Amber rolls her eyes. No sense pretending now. "Hi Dave."

"Yeah, I was trying to. It was more difficult than I thought it would be."

"Oh, ok." I say. "Well, um, ok. Yeah, that would be fun."

"Great! Thanks for calling, Rita. It was good talking to you...and to Amber!"

"Yeah. ok. See you Sunday, then. Um, bye?" I say as I hang up. Phew. That's done. I look at Amber. "Well that's done. You owe me and Andrew lots of pizza! That was horrible."

"Nope. I owe Andrew pizza. I think it took you 15 seconds to blush. I totally lost my bet with Andrew!" She pauses, then says, "Seriously, though, it might have been hard. But you're better for it. Aren't' you? Facing your fears?"

I refuse to acknowledge it. I don't want to think about that stilted, uncomfortable conversation. "So, go get Elias and Sarah and let's start this movie!"

Amber laughs. "Ok! We will need to talk about plans, though. No avoiding that!"

"Whatever. I'll just agree to whatever you decide. 'Cause I truly don't care. All I care about is getting yummy pizza. Right, Andrew?"

"Mmmmmmhmm," Andrew says.

I put my hand to my head as I remembered. "Oh, that's right, I need to give Andrew his medicine! Thanks for the reminder, Andrew!" I go to the Ramseys' kitchen and get a glass of water for Andrew while I hear Amber going up the stairs to the kid's rooms to get them to come down. I get Andrew's medicine out and put it in a bowl so it'll be easier to retrieve one at a time for him.

Amber is right. I know it was good for me to have that conversation. But thinking back to it, I just didn't like the way I wasn't "natural" around it. And thinking about how stupid I must have sounded didn't make it any better. But if that is the way our conversations are going to go, I'm not looking forward to prom night, either. Though, to be fair, it'll not just be the 2 of us. Amber will be there, too. So, I'm sure that will help. She'll carry the conversation for all 4 of us and make us all feel included, knowing her.

Just then I hear Elias and Sarah giggling as they are coming down the stairs. Sarah comes running into the kitchen, 'Hide me! Amber's gonna get me!"

I open up the cupboard door by the sink and let her crawl

in. I quickly shut it as Amber comes around the corner with Elias squirming in her grasp. "I've got one kid, I'm missing another. I need them both to fill my belly before the movie!"

Elias is giggling as he is trying to get out. "Nooo," he laughs.

"Where did the little girl go?" Amber asks in her fake gruff voice.

I shrug my shoulders as I walk past Amber with water and medicine. "No little girl here. I've just been here getting water and getting Andrew's medicine out."

Just then Sarah starts laughing from her hiding spot and Amber makes a big show of searching for her to finally "find" her. By the time I've given Andrew his medicine, Amber comes into the living room with both children, each laughing as she has them in her grasp. She gets them on the couch and then chooses the movie (insisting that the movie choice was Andrew's and mine.)

I agree that it was the movie we were dying to see and thanking them for letting us watch it. Both Elias and Sarah look at me and nod seriously, determined to be nice and not complain about what I chose to watch. Amber has a way with people, siblings included!

I look at Amber and mouth "Thank you." She nods her head in response. She knows it's not just this time with her and her family, though it's partly that. It's being a friend. It's looking out for me, and Andrew.

6 |

I settle into my seat in my Spanish class. I see Amber duck into the classroom just as the bell goes off. "Cutting it close, aren't you?" I say as she rushes to the seat next to me.

She laughs, "*Lo siento, Señorita.*"

I giggle. Our Spanish teacher always lets us chat for a few minutes before we start class. We are a small class and all seniors so she gives us a little more slack than she did in previous years.

"Are you nervous about tonight?" I ask her. Tonight is the night Amber's mom is taking her out to discuss the future, or whatever. Tonight is the 2nd Thursday in a row that Amber will miss our pizza nights.

"I am trying not to be. But I'm glad you and Andrew came over Tuesday. It was a lot fun, wasn't it?"

"Yeah, I know Andrew had a lot of fun. He giggled and danced the whole time I pushed him to your house."

"Yeah I think we should have you guys over more often, and you could use the exercise. You are getting sort of flabby!" She pauses. "Seriously, though, you should come over more often. By the time I had to put Sarah to bed, she was no longer looking at Andrew nervously."

"I know that was kinda exciting. Talking to Dave wasn't." I shudder as I remembered that awkward conversation.

"I dunno. It wasn't *too* bad."

I shake my head. "You know, lying doesn't suit you!" Just then Señora Classen claps her hands, signifying the start of class. Amber and I moved in our seats to face forward.

Amber always walks with me after our class. She heads to lunch this period. As we are walking to my next class we resume our conversation. It seems like all she wants to talk about now is Dave and I. I'm not even sure why; it's not like we're dating. We're just planning on going to the prom. That's it. I listen to her with half an ear as I remember that stilted phone conversation. Not for the first time in the last two days, I went over the conversation in my head and thought of all the things I should have said better, but didn't.

Since we all grew up in the church together, we have had years of getting to know each other. However, it's always been the three of us. And, this scenario was something neither Dave nor I were used to.

My mind comes back to the present as I arrive at my next class door. I say goodbye to her as I go in. I hope Amber didn't notice I wasn't really listening to her. Amber waves goodbye and heads to the cafeteria.

Three more classes to go, I think to myself as I sit down in my usual seat. At least tonight is pizza night again.

Silas waves at me as I walk by him to put my backpack

away. I smile in return. "How are you doing today?" I ask as I shove the backpack in its usual spot.

"Ok, I guess. For some reason it's been slow, not even 2 carts for you to put back. You'll be done earlier than usual, I think!"

"OK. Well, better get started then, huh?" I wheel the first cart over to the shelves. It's almost the end of the week and I start thinking about my plans with Rosa this weekend. I should check to see what the weather will be like on Saturday. It is pizza night, so I will have Andrew care, but I can check on my phone while we watch our movie. I realize that I don't even have homework tonight because we actually don't have *that* many days of school left. I just have the final project in creative writing, but I don't want to have to think about it tonight. To be honest, I think most of the teachers assume it'll be hopeless to get their seniors to do any sort of work at this point.

As I move on to the next row of books, I mentally calculate the days. I am surprised when I come up with the total. Only 25 more days of school left! I should make a paper chain and hang it up in my room--kind of like what I did as a kid counting down days until Christmas. I should make them alternating purple and white--our school colors. I wonder if we even have construction paper still?

I am considering where to hang the chain in my room when I realize that all of the books have been shelved already. I head back to Silas, pushing the cart. "You're right, I was done really quickly!" I say as I grab my backpack and throw it over my shoulder. "See you tomorrow, Silas."

He waves goodbye and I head to my chained bike.

When I arrive home, I put my bike away and head inside. Since I am home earlier than usual, Mom's not in frantic mode yet. She is currently sitting at our dining room table, and Andrew is in his wheelchair next to her. Mom looks up in surprise when I enter, "Home so soon?"

"Yeah, not very many books to shelve today. So I finished really quickly."

"Okay. Glad you get some extra time! Know what you and Andrew are going to watch tonight?"

"I think we'll watch *Wall-E*; it's been a while." *Wall-E* is his favorite, or at least our family thinks it's his favorite. Andrew will watch the movie in its entirety and do his excitement dance throughout the movie. I think it might be his favorite because it used to be *my* favorite movie (after I outgrew *Moana*, that is). As a result, we watched it a lot when he was younger.

"Sounds great!"

I go over to Andrew and kiss him on his head and sit down on the other side of my mother. "Hey, Mom. Do we have construction paper?"

Mom looks up to the ceiling as she tries to remember. "Maybe in a desk drawer in the office? If not there, I'd look in the closet in the office. Why?"

"Oh, figured I'd make a paper chain to countdown days of school! I can do it while we're watching the movie, maybe."

"Which reminds me," Mom says, raising her finger, "We should go this weekend to look for a prom dress."

I groan. I hate shopping--especially for clothes. "How does that remind you?"

"You were talking end of year, my mind went prom. It makes logical sense."

"If you say so. The only plans I have are with Rosa. We are taking Andrew to the lake in the afternoon."

"I'm sure he'll love that!" Mom squeezes my shoulder and she gets up from her chair. "Be excited about shopping! It'll be fun mother-daughter bonding!"

"Pfft, I'd rather bond over a pan of brownies."

"Hey, we can do that too!" Mom laughs and looks at her watch. "I guess I should start getting ready. I'll put the medicine on the counter for Andrew."

"Mom, you say it *every* week. I know!"

"I know, I know, but I have to say it. I think if I don't, the world will fall apart."

I roll my eyes. I get up as well to search for the construction paper.

I am sitting in my usual chair next to Andrew attaching my chain pieces. Andrew and I already ate our pizza and the movie is almost over. Andrew jiggles and shakes the chair. "Yeah, it's exciting isn't it, Andrew? Do you like the end?" I murmur as I tape a strip of purple paper into a circle.

My phone rings. I glance over at it and see it's from Amber. I smile and pick up. She had her meeting with her mom and I want to hear what happened.

"Hello?" I say. My smile quickly turns to shock and horror.

After the phone call is over, my phone drops from my numb hand and clatters to the floor.

7

I sit in the chair in the waiting room, my mind racing. Dave is sitting next to me, nervously drumming his fingers on his lap. Mr. Ramsey is sitting in the corner, looking very alone. I put my head in my hands and close my eyes; it's going to be a long night and I should try to rest if I can. "You can go, Dave," I offer for not the first time. "I can get a ride home later from my mom or dad. I've texted my parents; they know what is going on. No sense you losing more sleep than you already have." I open up my eyes to peer at him, but Dave just shakes his head. I know he's already texted his parents that it will be a while. I appreciate the gesture, though. I sigh and close my eyes again and try to process the whirlwind of the past few hours.

After Mr. Ramsey called earlier using Amber's phone, I was stunned for what seemed like forever, but I suppose it was only a minute or two. The first thing I did when I recovered my senses was to call my parents to ask them to come home. I was frantic and I'm sure they barely understood what I was saying. Heck, I barely understand *now* what's going on.

I knew I needed to visit Amber, so after calling my parents, I wanted to get a ride to the hospital. I guess I could have asked one of my parents to drive me, but I don't know. I wasn't really thinking clearly, I suppose. Looking back, I remember pacing after hanging up with my parents, mumbling to myself, "Who to call? Who to call?"

I settled on Dave. He knows Amber, and I was so upset I even forgot to be self-conscious in this conversation. I explained what little I knew and asked if he'd be willing to take me to the hospital once my parents came home.

Dave quickly agreed and said he'd come over. Dave beat my parents to the house. I was still pacing when he arrived. He actually made me sit down and got me a glass of water. He noticed Andrew in the middle of the room and the movie was well over. He asked me if there was anything he could do to help me with Andrew.

I must admit I had forgotten about Andrew. I think Andrew picked up on my emotions as he was quiet in his chair, barely making a sound. "Um, I need to get him ready for bed."

Dave nodded. "Ok, so what do I need to do?"

In another time, I maybe would've been surprised at this offer. I don't remember Dave ever making an effort to interact or even notice Andrew throughout the years our families have known each other.

"I need to change his brief and get him in his pajamas. Don't worry, I'll take care of it. I don't want to ask you to do it," I said as I got up. The simple fact of remembering my brother helped me calm my nerves and racing heart.

Dave followed me as I pushed Andrew into his bedroom. "Seriously, Dave. You don't need to help. I appreciate the offer but it's simpler if I just do it. Thank you for making me calm down," I said with a hitch.

Dave didn't say anything but still followed me into Andrew's bedroom.

My parents came home as I was getting Andrew's pajamas on. Dave was helping Andrew stand up while I was getting them situated. Mom rushed into the bedroom and gave me a hug. "Honey, go ahead, your dad and I will take it from here."

I smiled, trying not to cry, and stood up. Dave walked out of the house with me and I got in his car. I was nervous, worried, and upset the whole car ride. I stared out the window and didn't talk. We both rode in silence.

Once we parked, I hurried out of the car and he followed me. I knew right where to go because Mr. Ramsey told me when he called. We've been in the waiting room ever since.

I shift in my chair to be more comfortable. Even now, hours after, I don't want to think about what happened.

I make my mind go over the facts, as I know it. Apparently, Mrs. Ramsey was driving and they were turning left. A car hit them right at Amber's door. I don't know if the car is totaled, but from what I hear about Amber's injuries, I suppose it is. Mrs. Ramsey doesn't have as extensive injuries; the doctors say she has some bruising and whiplash but nothing too serious. Amber is another story. The doctors are keeping her immobile. She's had Xrays, an MRI, and I don't know what else. We haven't heard an update just yet. However, the doctors have told Mr. Ramsey that Amber has had a spinal cord injury. It will take a few days to determine how bad it is.

My mind goes back to my last conversation with Amber.

Was it really just this morning at lunch? I can't believe it. I wish I told her how much I loved her. I wish I told her how much she means to me instead of being slightly annoyed that she was still talking about Dave. I look at Mr. Ramsey. Is he doing the same thing as I am? Is he going over his day and wondering "If only..." as well? I'm not sure I want to interrupt his thoughts. I know I really don't want to talk but maybe knowing someone cares will help. I sigh and move over to the seat next to Mr. Ramsey. I hold his hand. I don't say anything, because I can't. Even if I wanted to talk, no words come to mind.

I see tears make paths down his cheeks and I squeeze his hand. With that squeeze, I hope he knows that I'm here, I understand. With that squeeze, I know I'm not alone in my grief.

In the early hours of the morning, Mrs. Ramsey is released. Dave and I offer to take her home so Mr. Ramsey can stay and await news on Amber. I give Mr. Ramsey a hug and I try to not cry as I say goodbye. "Let me know what you hear, please."

Mr. Ramsey nods his head silently. I turn around and put my arm around Mrs. Ramsey's shoulder to support her in her walking. We follow Dave out of the waiting room and to the elevator to the parking lot. Mrs. Ramsey is quiet. If not for the tight grip on my right arm, I'd not have known she was with us. When we arrived at the car, I help her into the back seat of the car. She starts to cry. "Oh, I'm sorry Mrs. Ramsey.

Did I hurt you?" I quickly look to see if there was something I did to cause her pain.

"It's my fault. It's my fault." She moans quietly to herself.

I look at Dave and say, "I think I'll sit next to her in the back." Dave nods his head and walks to the driver's side.

I settle in next to Mrs. Ramsey. I grab her hand and stroke it unconsciously like I do for Andrew. It seems to calm her down like it does for Andrew. She looks at me and says, tears streaming down her face, "It's my fault. Bill and I had a fight right before Amber and I left. I told Amber I wanted to drive. If I wasn't so upset, maybe I'd have seen the car. If I was paying attention, maybe my little girl would have been safe. I should've let her drive. It's my fault. It should've been me!"

I keep stroking her hand and make calming noises. I don't know how to comfort her. How do I without sounding like I'm spouting platitudes? Everything I can think of to say all sounds so trite. I settle on this, "We don't know what is in store the next few days. But I'm sure Amber will say that no matter what, she loves you."

Before long, Dave pulls into the Ramsey's driveway. I get out and walk around the car. I open up the door and assist Mrs. Ramsey out of the car. Jenny comes running out of the front door. "Any news? How's Amber?"

"Your dad is still waiting to hear. He said he'd let me know, and I'm sure you'll know before me. Your mom is in pain, but should be ok." Jenny comes and takes over assisting her mother into the house.

"How'd babysitting go last night?" I ask as I walk on ahead to open the screen door.

"Ok, I guess. We all were scared. Sarah and Elias took some convincing to go to sleep. But they're still sleeping, which is good." She glances at her phone, "Heh, it is 5am. So I guess it's not surprising they're still sleeping."

Once Jenny gets her mother settled in the recliner. She hugs her mother and kisses her on the head. "Mom, do you want anything?"

Mrs. Ramsey silently shakes her head. "Well, I should head home too, I guess." I give Jenny a quick hug. "Let me know if you need anything. I'm not going to school today, either."

Jenny agrees and I head out the door to Dave's car. He had gotten out of the car and was leaning against it, waiting. He looks so tired, his dark hair disheveled. I touch my hair and can tell a lot of hair has come out of my ponytail, so I guess I probably do too.

I get in the passenger side while he gets back into the car. "Thanks again for driving me and staying. I truly appreciate all the help you've given."

"It was no problem. I care about Amber, too, you know. Keep me posted when you hear news, please. Also, if you want a ride to the hospital again, let me know." he says as he pulls out of the driveway.

"Ok, thanks." I yawn. "I'm so tired, but I'm not sure I can even go to sleep."

He laughs and says, "I don't think I'll have that problem. I think I'll fall asleep as soon as I hit my bed."

Soon enough, he pulls into our driveway. My house is still dark, people won't be waking up for at least another hour or so. I give him a quick hug goodbye. "Thanks again for everything, Dave. Really. I can't thank you enough." I can tell my eyes are starting to tear up again and I quickly turn away. I don't know why. It's not like he didn't see me crying last night or even if it's a bad thing that I'm crying. But I guess it is reflex. I don't know. I fumble with the door handle and get out. After shutting the door, I wave goodbye again and mouth, "Thank you," and head into the house.

I hear him backing out of the driveway as I enter the door. I think back on the last few minutes. I gave him a hug. That's weird. I am usually so self-conscious around guys that I generally don't hug them. I shake my head. My best friend is in the hospital and in serious condition and I'm thinking about a guy. What kind of friend am I? I can remember Amber gushing about Dave yesterday and I wonder what she'd say about what just happened. I head over to my room trying not to think about last night and this morning. I get under the covers after kicking off my shoes and close my eyes as soon as I put my head on the pillow. Elgato comes to his normal spot by my bed and purrs as he curls up. I give him a small smile and fall asleep. *I guess Dave was right and I was wrong.*

8

I am sitting on my bed. After searching for an hour, I finally found my box of rocks that I collected with Amber. I was right and it was in the back of my closet. I'm not a very organized person and I have a tendency to never want to throw anything away. The perfect storm. I pick up a rock and turn it. I don't remember where or when I found this rock but it certainly is interesting. It has some purple and green specks dispersed throughout the rock. I look down at all the rocks and realize that I don't remember the stories behind any of them. This saddens me.

I had gotten a text from Mr. Ramsey about an hour ago now, from his phone. I made sure he had my number last night and put it in his contacts so he could easily text me. Amber is stable. They've confirmed that she has a spinal cord injury but they won't know the extent of the injury until a few more days. The doctors said she could have non-family visitors probably tomorrow. Mr. Ramsey said he was in her room now and will be there until tomorrow.

I get a text just then. My phone is charging at my desk and I can't see it from where I'm at. However, I figure it's not Mr. Ramsey. When last we texted, he said he'd give me an update this evening. I want to be alone with my thoughts. I miss my friend; I miss being able to talk to her. I feel selfish missing her. She's in the hospital and all I can think of is that I don't have my friend to talk to. Is that wrong? Am I only thinking of myself?

My phone pings again. I ignore it. I don't know who it is, but it's no one I want to talk to, anyway. I pick up another rock and peer at it.

My parents had quietly gotten Andrew ready for school and headed out the door to their respective jobs. My mom did leave a note saying she called the school and the library that I wasn't coming in. I appreciate that. I look at my clock and realize that my mom should be coming home soon. I throw myself down on my bed and close my eyes. Apparently that's Elgato's clue to come on the bed and take his spot on my bed. I giggle. "*No es hora de ir a la cama.*"

I open up my eyes and Elgato yawns. I guess he disagrees. I grab my book by my bed and figured I'd read. Maybe, just maybe, it'll get my mind off of everything.

After a few minutes, I give up trying. I read the same page 4 or 5 times without even knowing what I read. I stare at Elgato as he snuggles up to me. He is safe and secure and is happy. I crave for that contented feeling–to feel safe and secure no matter what. I want that, and if I'm honest, I don't think I have ever had that. I'm always worried about how I am perceived. I want people to be happy, and I don't want them to judge me. I don't want them to judge Andrew or my family. I'm tired. I want my friend. A hole is inside of me and I'm afraid. Just then, I hear my phone ping again.

I sigh. I guess I will read the texts. One from my mom, two from Dave. I read my mom's first.

Hi Honey, just checking in with you. How are you doing? Do you want anything? Ice cream? Chocolate? I can pick it up on my way home, if you want. Let me know.

I am not fine. But I don't want to share my feelings yet. I need to process them. I just send a quick text back that I am ok and no don't need anything.

I decide not to read Dave texts yet. I want to dwell on my pain right now. I don't want to explore my thoughts about Dave.

I close my eyes. My mind flits through images of times with Amber. No rhyme or reason. I see Amber the last time we met on the lake. I see an image of her and I inspecting a potato bug in her back yard when we were like seven. Amber in the 7th grade play. I was in the audience, her #1 fan. Reading our favorite book together side by side. We each had a mug of hot chocolate to the side of us. Pretending to be our favorite Warrior Cats in my backyard. Then, I see us at a youth group retreat–it was the time Dave, Amber and I were fishing. My mind stops there. It was my first time fishing. I cast my line and the fishing wire got caught in a nearby tree that had overhanging branches. Amber decided to climb the tree to undo the line. Her weight was too much for the branch, and she went into the lake. Dave fished her out. All three of us laughed over how Amber ungracefully fell into the water.

I give a half giggle out loud as I recalled that image. Elgato moves and I open my eyes to look at him. He is glaring at me for disrupting his sleep. I pat his head apologetically as I close my eyes again. My mind continues to sift through memories again as if it is cataloging "Times with Amber". I see the first time Amber and I met Elias, as a newborn at the hospital. I see the first time we met Sarah. Amber (and younger siblings) stayed with us. I see me half listening to Amber on the way to lunch. I remember her crying when her dog died. I remember her excitement when she opened last year's Christmas gift I had given her. The images my mind brings to the forefront are faster and faster and I feel my heart beating, as if to keep time with the memories.

I open my eyes to stop the mental images. Just then, I hear the front door open. It's my mom. I dread the conversation we will be having soon–how are you doing? Anything I can do to help? Need anything? I know why she will ask and check on me. But that still doesn't change the fact that I don't want it. I just want to be left alone.

My mom knocks on my door and then her head peers in. She glances around and takes in my emptied rock collection, me on the bed. "Hi, sweetie. How are you? Have you heard from Mr. Ramsey?"

I decide to answer the last question. "Yeah. She is stable. Mr. Ramsey said we can likely visit tomorrow. He will text tonight."

My mom quietly asks, "And you?"

I find a spot on the corner of my desk to look at so I won't have to make eye contact with her. "Ok, I guess."

My mom comes in and gives me a hug. As she does, she

whispers, "I love you. I'm here for you. Just let me know when you're ready."

I feel the tears coming again and I just nod my head.

Why am I ashamed of my emotions? Why can't I cry in front of people? Be snotty? Why am I always concerned about upsetting people?

I know Andrew will be home soon. I know I should get up and help Mom with Andrew. But I just can't. I can't will myself to get up and interact. I feel selfish. I know Mom's routine. Since I've started working, I've not been there to help her. But I have helped her for years.

She gets Andrew off the bus, brings him into the living room. She talks to him as she unloads his backpack from the wheelchair. She goes into the kitchen to get his medicine, and next she gives him his medicine. She then moves him to the table, so she can talk to him while she reads. Tonight is Friday, so Dad will be doing the cooking tonight.

My phone pings with a text. I glance at the clock, it's not evening, but maybe it could still be Mr. Ramsey? I'm half afraid to look in case it is an update. I grab my phone and see it's from Dave again.

The memory of fishing brought to mind that the three of us have been friends for so long. I realize he is worried and cares for her too. He would understand, more than anyone else, what I'm experiencing. Then I recall the hug last night. I blush. Why did I do that? It seems I always ruin things and make things weird. Amber always knew what to say and when to say it. Not me. But texting is better than in person, for sure. I sigh. I guess I'll read his texts.

I didn't sleep well. I'm worried about Amber. Hear any-thing?

I guess not. Just let me know if you do.

I don't want to talk to my parents or anyone else. I just want to talk with you. I know my pain doesn't compare with what you're going through. You two are so close. But I think only you will truly understand

I catch my breath. I feel the tension I didn't even know I had slowly release. I don't know why but I feel safe talking about this to Dave. Why didn't I read his texts sooner? I quickly type a response with the information I had, minimal though it is.

He and I text back and forth. In the background, I hear Dad making dinner, talking with Mom. Somehow, the hole I have doesn't seem so gaping. I'm not alone in this pain. In the back of my mind, I'm berating myself for being selfish and not realizing that other people might be hurting too. It just seems I never do it right. I wish I would. I'm tired of making mistakes and harming people in the process.

I hear a knock and Dad pokes his head inside. "Rita, dinner's ready if you want."

I look up from my phone and shake my head no. He nods and slips out the door.

Just then, I get a text from Mr. Ramsey. *Still stable. Doctors confirm that Amber can have visitors tomorrow.*

I copy and paste the message to Dave, and then to both my

parents. I know my parents would like to visit Amber, too. We need to make sure someone is home with Andrew. Until Amber is awake, it is probably best to have Andrew stay home since his wheelchair takes up a lot of room. Which means I have to coordinate with my parents. Ugh. A stray thought of frustration, aimed at Andrew, comes to mind. I quickly squash it. I love him, and I want what is best for him. I truly do. A good sister would never think those thoughts. Just adds to my mental list of mistakes.

Dave asks if I wanted a ride to the hospital tomorrow. I sigh. I guess I need to go talk to my parents.

I roll off the bed, causing Elgato to jump down from the bed. *"Lo siento,"* I apologize to him as I head out of my bedroom.

9

I am next to Andrew. As soon as my parents left to go visit Amber, I got him out of his chair and he and I are snuggling together on the couch. I am stroking his hand, while replaying the events of this morning.

Dave picked me up and took me to the hospital. The car ride with Dave both to (and from) the hospital was quiet. Neither of us talked. But it wasn't an awkward ride. I felt comfortable just thinking my thoughts and not feeling the need to talk. After my trip down memory lane yesterday afternoon, I retrieved our favorite childhood Warrior Cats book, *Moth Flight's Vision*. (I may be disorganized in all other areas, but my books are always neat and tidy on my bookshelf.) As we made our way to her room, I had the book clasped tight to myself, almost like I was hugging Amber. I wished I was hugging her! When I entered the room, it was bright and cheery, except for the banged up patient in the bed. Her dad was on the other side of the bed, slumped in a chair. It looked like he was running on fumes. I'm sure he hasn't had much sleep. I realized just then I had been so focused on Amber, I didn't even think to check up on Amber's mom. I came in and sat in the one other chair by Amber's bed and grabbed her hand.

She was sleeping. I stroked her hand like I do with Andrew. I told her I loved her. I explained where I found my rock collection box but I couldn't remember any of the stories behind the rocks. I'd need her help to remember. I placed the book to her side. I remember telling her, while trying to hold tears back seeing her, "I brought this for you. To keep you busy when you wake up. It was our favorite book! I'm still mad you made me read it! I didn't like what happened to Micah!" I quickly ran out of things to say because I didn't know what to say. She looked so helpless and frail. It was like she wasn't really Amber. Even her blonde curls seemed lifeless. The girl on the hospital bed was just a shell of Amber.

I looked around the room and just then realized Dave was standing quietly at the foot of the bed. I got up to let Dave take the chair and then I went over to Mr. Ramsey. I asked about his wife and Amber's siblings. Apparently they all got to visit Amber last night but Amber's mom is still recuperating–physically and mentally. I just stood there quietly next to him while Dave talked quietly to Amber. I found a spot on the wall to focus. It was a tiny tree that was in the picture across from me. I don't know why I do that when I'm bored, or when I am uncomfortable. I just stare at something and focus on that, rather than what I am trying to avoid. Does everyone do this? Or am I just weird? I don't know if I'll ever find out. It's not like you can strike up a conversation and say "Hey, do you stare at things when you don't want to pay attention?" I half laugh to myself. Saying it like that, it doesn't even make sense.

Just then, Andrew starts moving side to side and saying

"Mmmmmm". He does this when he is happy. I smile and lean forward and give him a hug. "I love you, Andrew! I'm enjoying sitting here too!"

Glancing at the clock on the wall, I realize it's approaching lunch time. I get Andrew back in his chair and wheel him to the table. I talk to him from the kitchen as I'm preparing our lunch. After lunch I'll give him his medicine. I start preparing grilled cheese sandwiches for us, because it seems to be his favorite. Plus I like them too!

I bring the grilled cheese sandwiches to the table and when Andrew sees the plate he starts moving side to side so much the wheelchair rocks a little bit. "Hold on, Andrew," I laugh. "I promise you'll get the grilled cheese, just let me sit down first!"

Once we are finished, I clean up and start getting his medicine out. I realize as I do this, I didn't think about Amber the last hour or so. Does that make me a bad friend? My friend is in the hospital and I should be thinking about her. I know it makes no sense, but a part of me thinks what is happening to her is my fault. I didn't pay attention to her the last time we talked. Maybe if I had, nothing bad would have happened to her.

I give Andrew his medicine. I glance outside. "Let's go outside, Andrew. Maybe take a short walk around the block?"

I leave a note on the table in case Mom and Dad come back while we are gone. I push him out and make sure to lock the door behind me.

Rosa is outside tending to her garden in purple and orange this time. She stands up when she notices us. "Hey, Rita and

Andrew!" she greets us. "Do you want to go to the lake now? I just need to get my walking shoes on!"

That's right! We had set a time to go to the lake to learn flowers this afternoon. It was like time stopped when Amber had her accident. It seemed like forever ago but it really it was only 2 days ago. I didn't want to go back to my "normal" life. However, I know it'd be good for Andrew to be outside. I glance at the sky, it was clear and kind of sunny. I suppose I should get us some sunscreen if we're going to be outside for that long. "Sure, Rosa. I'll just run inside and get some sunscreen for Andrew and I. Meet you out back on the path?"

Rosa gives a thumbs up and we both go back inside. Rosa knows Amber just from the fact that Amber is at the house so often. There's no way she'd have known Amber had the accident. I'm not sure I can tell her. I am not ready to share my feelings–even with someone who knows our family so well.

I get the spray sunscreen. I like it better than the lotion. The greasiness of the lotion makes me feel so gross. The spray is easier to apply on Andrew too. We are ready in a just a few minutes. I edit the note to my parents that we will be at the lake instead and then I wheel Andrew out the back door. It's hard to push him through the pathway until we get to the paved path. But the distance is pretty short. When we get there, Rosa is waiting for us. She sees us and gives both of us a huge smile. "Hey, Andrew! Ready to see all the beautiful flowers?? We are going to see so many. I wonder which one will make you smile more?"

I smile as I see her talking to Andrew. It is so nice to see someone engaging with Andrew. Yes, he can't talk back but he enjoys being around people. Just like anyone, he likes to be noticed, to be seen.

Rosa glances at me. "Rita, you ready? You better pay attention, there will be a quiz after!" She laughs as she leads the way. I smile. I'm glad we are here. The sun is warm. The flowers are pretty and it's nice to be doing "normal" things. I know if Amber were not in the hospital, she'd want to do this very thing with us. That thought somehow makes it easier to proceed. I'm doing this for Amber.

I walk back with Andrew, a little disappointed that I definitely failed the quiz. I did not receive the prize of a chocolate chip cookie. Andrew did, though! The dork. I think I correctly identified two of the flowers we saw at the lake when we came back to Rosa's place. I will need to study some more. Amber probably would have gotten a 100 and maybe gotten an extra credit somewhere (I don't know how, but she has a tendency to do it!). I have a huge bag of cookies in hand for our family.

When we come back home, I see Mom and Dad had returned. "Hey guys," I greet as I wheel Andrew in backwards.

Mom comes in and gives the both of us hugs. "Hi! How was the lake? How was Rosa?" I tell her about the time and the fact that I definitely didn't pass the quiz. I then show her the bag of cookies. "Aww that was so sweet of Rosa! Her cookies are so good!"

I agree. They are the best. I don't know how she does it, but they are so good. She swears all she uses is the premade dough. But when I bake cookies with the premade dough they never turn out so soft and chewy like hers.

I kiss Andrew on the head as I take the cookies to the kitchen. I sneak one as I place it on the counter. I head to my room. I can't believe how that walk changed my outlook. I'm still sad and worried about Amber, but doing something normal helped me just put things in perspective somehow. Life goes on. Sometimes it sucks, but it still moves on. And somehow that is comforting to me.

I pull out my phone from my back pocket. I had it on silent from when I was at the hospital and forgot to put it back on. Now I realize I had missed quite a few texts from Dave. There is a text from a friend of mine in creative writing class. Tiffany is a senior as well. She and I are supposed to do a final project together; it's due soon. Tiffany and I are supposed to write a children's book, with illustrations. I was glad we were paired up. Tiffany draws really well. Me? I draw stick figures. And, to be completely honest, some of the 3 year olds that draw on the paper provided at the library draw better than I.

Our high school is large enough that I don't know everyone in my class. But I can recognize most people by sight, anyway. However, I can pretty much guarantee most people know who Amber is. She is likely to be the valedictorian of the class. I look at Tiffany's text and she is asking when we can get together to work on the story. I'm tired already. It was an emotional and tense morning. People wear me out. I enjoyed my time at the lake but that added to it. I text that maybe tomorrow afternoon we could do it over the phone, rather than in person. Tiffany agreed and we settle on a time.

I glance through Dave's texts. He was wanting to chat, talk about this morning. I feel bad. I feel like I'm being very selfish and only focused on my pain. And he's been the one to drive me back and forth to the hospital twice. I need to be a better friend to him.

I apologize for the missed texts, told him about our trip to the lake and asked how he was doing. I don't know why, but my reticence of interaction with Tiffany doesn't apply to Dave. If I can get over my shyness (which I can do via text), I truly do enjoy talking to him. I've known him most of my life. But usually Amber was around. I have come to find out from the past couple of days, though, we think very similarly. It's been good to have someone understand me so well.

In the midst of our texting conversation, I see a text from Mr. Ramsey. I read the first few words. At first I'm happy, then my heart sinks. I tap over to read the whole message. It isn't a surprise, but still hard to read. *Amber is awake. She has no feeling in her legs. Doctors think it is not likely she will walk.*

10

I'm in church. Sitting in the pew in the back with my family. I'm nervously tapping my foot. I just can't sit still because I'm afraid that if I do, I'll start thinking about Amber. I don't want to cry. Not in public.

I start counting the squares on the ceiling. It was what I did as a child when I was bored sitting in church. I'm not listening anyway and this meaningless task will help me not think. I start in the same corner I always did and start to count.

At last the pastor is doing the benediction. I start to quietly gather my things so that as soon as he says "Amen" I can get Andrew out of the sanctuary. Instead of my usual spot by the big window, I've already decided to just take Andrew to the van and wait there. The congregation starts moving and milling around. I lean over and ask my dad for the keys to the van and start wheeling Andrew over.

As I do, I allow myself to think. Mr. Ramsey said in the text that Amber has no feeling in her legs. I found out in following texts that she is going to be transferred to rehabilitation in the next couple of days and may be in rehab for a while –like months a while. I don't know how this will affect her graduation and her plans for school next year. Mr. Ramsey said Amber will likely be less sedated today, so I think I might text her. But what can I say? I know all the platitudes. I know Mom and Dad have even now said that God is control. He has a plan. There will be good that comes from this. Maybe there will. But right now I'm not seeing it. With Andrew, I grew up with him in a wheelchair. How can I get used to Amber in one? Will our friendship change because of it? I hope not. But I don't know the future. I still haven't figured out what my first message to Amber will be. All I can think of is "I love you and miss you." Will that be sufficient? I don't think it does my feelings justice but I honestly don't know what will.

We get to the van, Andrew and I. I unlock it as tears start to trickle down my face. I quickly wipe them away as I start the lift. I'm operating the lift when Dave comes to the van. I am not surprised he found me. It's kinda hard to miss our van–it stands out. No other wheelchair vans. Oh no! That thought hit me, almost like a punch. There will be another in the parking lot for the Ramseys. My tears start to fall more. I am trying not to sob.

Dave knows. When I got the message from Mr. Ramsey, I copied and pasted to parents and Dave once again. I quickly ended the conversation with Dave last night. I needed to process the news. It still is not processed.

"Hey, Rita. Hey, Andrew," Dave says.

I nod in greeting, not trusting my voice. I know it's obvious I'm crying. For some reason that he knows I'm crying doesn't bother me. It bothers me even if my parents know I'm crying. The only other person that I felt safe to cry in front of is Amber. This new relationship, this deepening friendship with Dave, is just weird. I still am afraid to talk to him in person (not just when I'm crying), it's just awkward and stilted. But apparently, I have no qualms about him seeing me at my snotty nosed, red eyes worst. How odd is that?

Dave hops inside the van and sits next to where I am. He gives me a gentle side hug. I glance over and he looks ahead through the windshield and starts talking. I laugh quietly to myself. He looks off too. "I know this is the last thing on your mind. But I wanted to let you know, we don't have to go to the prom. I thought, instead, we should visit Amber that night. She won't be able to go and I thought we could bring the prom to her. Bring music and yummy food at least."

Wow. I hadn't even thought of prom . But he is right. Amber won't be able to go to the prom and I certainly wouldn't want to go with her still in rehab, recuperating. I fish out a kleenex from a pocket behind the driver's seat. I blow my nose. (I'm not embarrassed to do that either in front of him!) "Yeah, I like that idea. Thank you, Dave."

He nods his head and just sits there quietly, each of us occupied with our own thoughts. I appreciate that. I glance around and notice the parking lot is getting pretty empty. "Do you need to go catch up with your family? They might have already left without you."

He shakes his head no. "I drove myself. I wasn't sure if you'd want to visit Amber now."

I half laugh. "I would love to visit her but I don't think I should go into the hospital looking like this. All the patients would run away in fear."

He lightly touches my hand. "Don't do that."

I don't move my hand. I like the contact, which is weird. "Do what?"

"Shortchange yourself. You have a lot to offer. And I'm sure a lot of people go to the hospital with tears and snot."

Yeah, he's right. But no one looks like I do with tears and snot. Whatever. "Ok. I have to talk to Tiffany today about a project in class. How about I text you when we are done. Do you mind?"

"No that is fine." Just then my parents came around the corner.

"I guess we are going now. Thank you, Dave. Talk to you later."

When my parents get to the van, they greet Dave as he leaves. We settle in our seats and head home. My parents are talking quietly back and forth between the two of them, which is fine with me.

I'm not hungry so as soon as we get Andrew out and in the dining room, I just head to my room. I text Tiffany to get the project started. I don't even have any ideas for a children's story. The only thing I'm thinking about these days probably isn't good material for a children's story!

After a few minutes she responds and we opt to just talk, rather than text. So, I call her. I could tell she knows about Amber. You know that awkward pause when someone knows something but they don't know how to bring it up? Tiffany initially tries to figure out what to say. So, I just let her know how things are with Amber. No sense beating around the bush, in my opinion.

Once done (and I didn't cry!), we discuss ideas. Well really we discuss ideas of Tiffany's. She apparently put a lot of thought into the project already. We settle on one—a hamster family going on a vacation. Since she is the artist, she will draw the pictures. I tell her I will try to write the story in the next few days so she can determine what pictures to draw. The hope would be to finish the project next weekend. We hang up and I text Dave.

I'm done with Tiffany. When do you want to visit Amber?

I decide to go ahead and text Amber what I was thinking earlier today, even if it doesn't convey the full range of emotions. To be honest, I don't think it is humanly possible to do so, especially since I have no idea what my full range of emotions are right now. A jumbled mess. But everyone likes to know they are loved and missed. I send the message as I wait to hear back from Dave.

I look around my room while I'm waiting to hear back. I see my rock collection strewn about on the floor by the foot of the bed. I guess either I knocked the rocks down in my sleep or Elgato used them as toys. I sigh. I should at least put them back in their box so I don't lose them. I think again how I wished I remembered the stories behind each one. Maybe I'll bring them to Amber to see if she remembers. Not today, though.

I glance at my phone to make sure it's not on silent. Why hasn't Dave texted me yet? I'm sure Dave felt this way on Friday and Saturday when I took a while to respond to his texts. He wouldn't purposefully not respond for that reason, right?

I get up off the bed and kneel down by the box and start to gather the rocks. Just then, Elgato comes out from under the bed and decides to rub up against me while I'm collecting the rocks. I laugh as he does. I immediately feel bad for laughing. Should I be laughing when my best friend is in the hospital and may never walk again?

Once my menial task is done, I turn so I can lean against my bed. I gather Elgato to my lap and he is happy to oblige. I lean back and close my eyes, petting my cat all the while. I know being a teenager is supposed to be confusing. But I think back to me this time a week ago, and it is like I've aged 5 years. Week-ago-me didn't know what it's like to be afraid for your friend's life. Week-ago-me didn't have these confusing thoughts about Dave. Week-ago-me didn't have to worry about what to say to Amber. I was so innocently blissful then.

A ping disrupts my mental monologue, thankfully. I open my eyes and search for my phone. I left it on my nightstand. It is Dave! He wasn't ignoring me, after all.

11

I glance at the sky as I walk to Dave's car. It's cloudy and kind of grey. I slip into the passenger seat when Dave arrives. I let Mom and Dad know we were visiting Amber. Mom was frantically making dinner to take over to the Ramseys. I guess there's a signup for church to bring meals and she chose today. I felt bad. I am sure she could have used my help. Instead, Mom gave me a hug and a $20 bill. She told me to get Amber some flowers or something for her room.

"Can we stop by a grocery store or something? Mom gave me some money to get Amber some flowers," I ask as Dave starts backing up from our driveway.

"Sure," Dave says. He brakes before he is out on the street to adjust his directions on his phone. Once set, he resumes pulling out of the driveway.

Things are quiet in the car, comfortably so. After a few minutes, Dave asks, "Do you know if Amber has a favorite flower? I don't know much about flowers, but we can certainly try to find it at the store."

"No. But she's always liked the really vibrant colors. So I guess some sort of arrangement with lots of bright colors." I pause and then state, " I don't know much about flowers, either. Although Rosa, my neighbor, attempted to teach me yesterday."

I am still talking about yesterday as we are heading into the grocery store. I quickly get the money I had stuffed in my pocket. We look around for a few minutes and I settle on a nice arrangement that has a small vase with a teddy bear. I figure she would like that the most. If not, she can always give the teddy bear to Sarah, I suppose.

After paying, we head back to the car. Dave turns on the car and plugs in the hospital address. I get settled with the flowers, trying not to damage them in any way. They are very pretty. It'll look nice and cheery in Amber's room, I think. I'll have to take a picture to send to Mom; I make a mental note.

I realize then that Amber never responded to my text. Not that it needed a response, but usually she at least responds with an emoji or something. I glance at my phone to double check and nothing. I wonder if she's awake, after all.

Before long, we arrive at the hospital and we make our way to Amber's hospital room. I knock on Amber's door and open it. It's dimly lit. I can see her watching tv, but the tv is on mute. I glance around and I don't see anyone else in the room. "Hey, Amber! Dave and I are here. We have flowers. Where would you like them?"

Amber turns her head and looks at me. She doesn't smile and oh her eyes have such sadness and pain. I hurriedly place the flowers on the counter by the sink and rush over to Amber. I give her a hug. "I've missed you so much! I'm so glad you're awake." I say, trying not to cry.

"I wish I could go back to sleep. I don't want to be awake

for this nightmare, Rita. I can't walk!" Amber looks away. My heart goes out to her. I don't know what to say.

Dave steps close to the hospital bed on the other side. He pulls up one of the chairs. "Rita was telling me in the car about how she failed a flower test yesterday."

Amber looks back and queries, "A flower test? What is that??"

Her interest piqued, I sit on the bed next to her and grab her hand and start to tell her about Rosa and the adventure. As I talk, I see Amber showing interest but still there was so much pain. I wish I could take it away for her. She has so much promise. Being a wheelchair won't stop her, I know it. But her life and her plans do have to change. My heart breaks for her.

My story done, Amber gives a small little smile. I start unconsciously stroking her hand, like I do for Andrew. Amber doesn't ask questions but she listens as I tell her stories about Elgato and the things I have seen at the library recently. I pause and then resume. "I have a project to do with Tiffany for creative writing. We are supposed to write a children's book together. We settled on a family of hamsters going on vacation. But, I can't think of where they should be going on vacation. Any ideas?"

At the mention of Tiffany, Amber took her hand away and bit her lip. "I don't want to help you with your school project! I can't believe you'd bring up school, right here and now. I don't even know if I'll graduate since I am going to be stuck in a hospital room for who knows how long! How could you, Rita?"

I am dumbfounded. I didn't even think how that might have sounded to Amber. For a moment, I had forgotten why we were here and just settled back into how we always talked and related. How could I be so stupid?

As I search for words, Dave tries to alleviate the tension in the room by changing the subject. "Have you seen Elias, Sarah and Jenny today? We chose the one we did because we thought Sarah might like the teddy bear."

"Yes, they came earlier today. It was good to see everyone." Dave nods and asks follow up questions, while I listen. I don't trust myself to come up with a neutral topic of conversation. The tension I've been holding in for the past few days is coming to a head. I can feel it. I know I'm going to just throw something or cry until my face melts from all the tears and snot or all of the above. I just know that I don't want to add to Amber's pain, so I'm attempting to keep the emotions in check.

Dave glances at me and I think he can tell that I'm about to lose it. He glances at his phone to check the time. "Amber, sorry. Rita and I have to go. My mom needs the car and I need to take Rita back. It is so good to see you! We will come back and visit, I promise." He gives her a quick hug. I lean over and hug Amber. I whisper "I love you" in her ear and give her an extra strong hug before standing up. I wave goodbye and follow Dave out the door.

I'm wiping tears as we walk through the hallways to the parking lot. I am looking at the floor so as to not make eye contact with anyone. At last, we get in Dave's car and I quickly shut the passenger door. I immediately start sniffing, looking for something to wipe my nose with–a napkin, paper towel, anything! Aha! I found some napkins in the glove box. I grab a couple as Dave settles in and plugs my address in the phone. I look out my window as I wipe my nose. Glancing at the wet streets, I guess it rained while we were outside.

"I'm sorry Amber reacted the way she did. She is dealing with a lot emotionally; I can't even imagine. But don't blame yourself for her reaction."

"It was dumb of me to bring up something school related. I just talked with her like I normally do. I should have realized."

Dave, waiting at a red light, looks at me. I can feel it. I continue to look out my window. "Question. If it were me that had asked, would you have been upset and tell me I'm stupid for not realizing?"

I snort my nose at the idea. "No. You wouldn't have known."

"Why do you expect you to have known?"

"Because Amber has been my best friend for years; I should be able to know."

Dave, driving through the intersection, asks quietly, "I'm her friend for years. Not best friends, I know. But shouldn't I have known?"

I shrug my shoulders. Then realize he might not have seen. "I don't know. I guess."

"I don't pretend to know Amber's thoughts and feelings. But I can imagine that she's going through a lot and is definitely grieving. But, you aren't responsible for her emotions. I think you take on too much responsibility; you think you need to keep everyone happy. You are a very kind and generous person. It's one of the many positive qualities you have. However, you should give yourself the grace you would have given me. You could not have known. You did your best."

The tears come down more after hearing that. Ugh. I hate that I do this. I nod my head, and get a weak "thanks" out. Really? Do I do that? The idea of giving myself grace is so new to me, but the thought that I could do so resonates with me. Can I do that? Can I allow myself the freedom to make mistakes? How would that even look?

The car slows down and I realize that we are almost home. Dave is pulling on to my street. "Thanks for driving me, Dave."

"I was glad to see Amber awake today. But no problem. Anytime you want to visit, just let me know. Will you be going to school tomorrow?"

"I don't know. Probably. Friday was hard. Maybe going to school will make the time go by quicker?"

Just then, Dave pulls into my driveway. I gather my things, well mostly just make sure my snotty napkins are picked up. "I know you didn't ask me. But I think you should have the story be after a favorite vacation you have had with your family. Write what you know, right? Or, at least, so I've heard."

Well duh. I should have thought of that. Dang! I catch myself. I just need to be grateful for the idea, not castigate myself for not thinking of it.

"Thanks, Dave. That's a good idea." I get out and shut the

door. If I do this change of attitude towards myself; it's going to take a lot of work. A lot of patience for myself. The one person I do not have patience for!

12

"Are you ready, sweetie?" Mom asks as I gather up my rock collection box.

"Yeah." I give Elgato a pat on the head as I leave the room.

"Andrew is already in the van. Your dad and Dave are getting him buckled in."

"Ok," I say as I follow her out the door. We're all going to visit Amber today. It was something I wanted to do. Amber loves Andrew and I still want to ask if she remembers the stories behind the rocks.

I'm nervous because this is the first time I'll have seen her since the fated time I brought up the children's story. That was three days ago. Amber is now in the rehab facility and I wanted to make sure she was settled in before we bombard her with our slew of people. Amber and I had texted a few times but I'm not sure how weird this time will be.

I quit my job. I went to work on Monday and told Mr. Silas it'd be my last day. I explained the situation and he was very understanding. I just want to be available to visit Amber as much as I can.

According to Mr. Ramsey, she is still struggling emotionally. Not surprising, though. Tomorrow will be one week since her accident. Even though this week seems like it has dragged on for forever, it really has only been seven days. Crazy.

I follow Mom out the door. I head to van as she locks the door. I climb in and sit next to Dave. "Hey, Dave. Thanks for coming with us."

"Sure thing. Thanks for letting me come along." He glances at my box that is in my hand. "What is that?"

"Oh, this is my rock collection box. When Amber and I were kids we each had a rock collection. I was looking through this box the other day and I could not remember a single story behind any of them. I was hoping maybe Amber would recall." I pause. "Maybe going down memory lane would be good for her right now, instead of worrying about what's around the corner."

"Yeah, maybe."

This conversation makes me recall the conversation I had with Amber just over a week ago, when she had me call Dave. She encouraged me to face my fears. I know having an awkward conversation pales in comparison to the fears she is facing, but perhaps I can encourage her like she encouraged me.

I bite my lip, trying to figure out how I might say it or bring it up. I don't know. Maybe having all these people wasn't a good idea. I have no idea how I can bring it up. *I just need to give myself grace. I am not in charge of Amber's emotions. I can try to help her, but ultimately it is her choice. Not mine. I can make mistakes. It's ok.* It is so hard to break the habit of *thinking*. However, it is worth it. I already have felt a lot less tension, as a whole. Just in the three days since

Dave and I talked about it. I tap the box. "I'm not sure if it'll help. But we will see. Who knows?"

Dave smiles and says, "Yeah, that's the spirit!"

Dad pulls into the parking spot and we all pile out of the van. Dad pushes Andrew into the rehab facility and I am holding Andrew's hand. He is excited and squealing as we go down the hallway; he always loves going to new places.

"What room was it again?" Mom asks as she pushes the handicap button that automatically opens the door.

"Um," I pull out my phone and check Mr. Ramsey's texts, "115."

We follow the signs to 115 and I knock on the door. We don't hear anything. I knock again, a little louder. Still nothing. Maybe she's sleeping? I open the door gingerly, "Amber? Amber?"

Amber turns her head towards the door. "Hi Amber. Dave, Andrew and my parents are all here. Can we come in?"

"Ok."

So we all pile in. Dad pushes Andrew close to the bed and then he and Mom stand back. I sit next to Amber. "Hi. How do you like your new room? It seems a bit bigger."

"Yeah it's ok."

Andrew, on seeing Amber, starts dancing in his chair. He has always loved Amber. "Andrew's definitely excited to see you. I am a tad bit jealous. He never greets me like he does you."

"Or us!" adds Mom

"Yeah, or Mom and Dad, true!" I laugh.

Amber smiles and reaches out her hand to hold Andrew's.

"Hey buddy. How you doing? You keeping Rita in line? You tell me if she does anything stupid?"

"Mmmm"

"Yeah, I know. I'm sure she keeps you on your toes!"

"Hey!" I say. "That's not fair!"

I can see a little bit of the old Amber light coming back into her eyes as she laughs. She definitely seems to enjoy seeing Andrew. *Yay! I'm glad I made the suggestion to Mom about having us all go today.*

I recall that I have the box in my lap. "Hey, Amber. I was looking for this box the other day after we mentioned it by the lake. I found it and it *was* at the back of my closet. But, I was wondering if you remember any of the stories of the rocks. I honestly can't remember a single one."

Amber reaches out her hands to grab the box. I place it in her hands. She pulls out a couple of rocks and looks at them. After the 3rd one she exclaims, "I remember this one!"

It is the very same one I looked at the other day, the one with purple and green specks. "Yeah? Where is it from?"

Dave pipes up, "Isn't that the one you found walking back from the lake, when Amber fell into the lake? I think Amber said it reminded her of a fish she saw in the lake or something."

"Yeah!" Amber agrees, "And then you said what I saw was probably Loch Ness or something. I dunno. We were like ten!"

I laugh, "Well, I remember you falling in the lake but not the rock! I'm glad you two remember. At least one mystery is solved. Remember anything else?"

After a few more tries, she holds up one. It is a rather large one and it isn't super sparkly. I'm sure it was chosen for its shape. It is roughly the shape of a heart.

"I remember finding this by the lake. You were sick with the flu or something. I was walking to your house with my mom, I think. I saw the rock and wanted to give it to you to cheer you up. You were so sick, I don't think you even were awake when I gave it to you."

"Awww. That's so sweet. I wish I remembered that."

"Yeah. I remember being so scared that you were dying or something."

I clear my throat. It was hitting a bit too close to home after this last week. "Well, I'm glad I didn't. And I'm glad you're my friend!" I reach out for her hand and squeeze it. She squeezes back.

I look up and see my mom and dad. "Mom, Dad, come closer. I'll move so you can." I get up and step back so they have a chance to visit. I need a minute anyway to calm my emotions.

Mom and Amber are chatting about something innocuous. How comfortable socks can be? Or something? I don't know. Mom has a great way to just make people feel comfortable. I have always wished I could be like that. Know just what to say and how to say it to make someone feel "at home." Amber has that ability too.

I do much better typing or writing something out. Then it hit me. Maybe I can just write her the message I was trying to think to fit in the conversation. About facing fears or something. Oooo and I can use the secret code she and I came up with as kids! Happy to have figured it out, I determine to text it in the van heading home.

I look around the room and saw that it really was a nice room. I see the Warrior Cats book I brought the last visit sitting on her nightstand by her bed. I wonder if she has read it yet?

Now Dad is talking to Amber. I definitely inherited my talking skills from my dad. I think the conversation lasted maybe 2 mins. They stand up and beckon me to sit by the bed again. I happily oblige. Dave and Amber are talking again about that retreat when Amber fell in the lake. I just listen and I'm glad to hear Amber having an animated conversation. It's so different than Sunday's conversation. It warms my heart to hear.

Mentally I compose the text I am planning on writing. I don't want it to be too long. I am holding her hand again and I feel her squeeze my hand. I squeeze back.

There is a lull in the conversation and my dad pipes in, "Well, we need to head back home and get Andrew medicine and dinner. Thanks for letting us all crash and visit. It's great to see your new room and see you again, Amber. I know Andrew loved it too!"

Andrew does his dance as my dad wheels him out. "I'll start getting him in the van."

"Well, I guess that's our cue to say goodbye, Amber. It was great to see you," Mom says as she comes in to give Amber a hug goodbye.

"Yeah. It was great to see you and fun to talk about that retreat with you!" Dave agrees as he hugs her good bye.

"Guess it's my turn," I say as I stand up. I retrieve the box from her lap but give her the heart shaped rock. "Here, take this. Until you're out of the rehab facility. I love you and I'm so glad you're my friend."

Amber holds the rock in her left and gives my hand a final squeeze with the right. "Ok. I'm glad you are mine."

I, once again, am leaving her room crying. This time for a good reason. I have my friend back. She isn't going to always be happy. But she is still my Amber and I'm so glad.

We get to the van, and Dad already has the van running and Andrew all set. We pile in. After I sit down, I pull out my phone and start my text. Remembering to add the secret code, I hit send.

13

I pull out the list I made, to make sure I don't forget any-thing else. It's the end of class and the end of day. No one's paying attention, least of all the teacher! Mr. Whitley is at his desk, reading emails or something. I don't know. I glance at my list again. Amber would be proud of me! I wrote a list down. I'll need to make sure to bring the list so she can see proof; I jot at the end of the list "Bring list". I don't know why that made me laugh to myself, but it did.

Tonight is prom. All the upperclassmen in my class (which is most of my class) are talking about it. We are doing what Dave suggested that one day after church. We are bringing the prom to Amber. I glance over to where Jeremy is sitting and I can't help but glare at him. When he found out that Amber couldn't go to the prom, he decided to ask someone else. The jerk.

A lot has happened in the last few weeks. I make a bulleted list in my mind. Bullet #1: Dave and I have visited Amber almost every day after school. Bullet #2: Amber said she ap-preciated the text I sent. It helped her change her attitude. Bullet #3: Amber has done really well at the rehab facil-ity. She's maneuvering well with the wheelchair and getting stronger. Understandably she still is grieving. However, she is doing much better mentally. I'm glad to have my friend back. It was hard seeing her in so much pain, both mentally and physically, at the beginning.

Amber will not be ready to walk the stage for graduation, but she's been told she will graduate. She just won't be valedictorian. She has high enough grades in all her classes, that even if she didn't turn anything in, she'd still pass her senior year. However, Amber has continued to turn in assignments, because she is Amber. She will continue to do so until the last day of school, knowing her. AP tests are around the corner, and she likely will not be healed enough to take them. She might not be okay with it, but she is resigned to it. I guess in that matter, she's grown too.

And Dave? Well, we've become closer friends. The more I get to know him, the more I realize we are more alike than anyone else I know. How could I have not noticed after so many years? Mom thinks he's my boyfriend. But we've not had any dates or anything. I've just really enjoyed getting to know him better.

Just then, the bell rings. Everyone stands up and heads to the door. I quickly put the list away. I slip through the doorway and head outside to my bike. I glance outside. It's sunny and bright. It's not too hot yet, perfect weather for biking home.

Dave and I went to the store last weekend to get decorations, paper products, and food. Those are all organized in bags in my room. My room is still a bit of a mess. I've grown, but not that much!

Mom wanted to still go shopping and get a prom dress. I said no. I didn't want to go to the hospital wearing a super fancy dress. I figured I'd wear the dress we bought for my cousin's wedding last year. It's nice but not super formal.

As for Amber's dress, Amber's mom found it online. Amber wouldn't let me see it. Yesterday we had stopped at the Ramseys to visit with them. I've been so focused on Amber, I realized I haven't visited Amber's siblings or parents. As I walked through the familiar hallways of the Ramsey home, I greeted each of the members. Mrs. Ramsey was mostly healed from her injuries, but she still blames herself for her daughter's injuries. When I greeted her, though, she did smile at me. The Ramseys hadn't been to church since the accident. I don't know why. Amber hasn't told me and I didn't want to pry and upset her.

I arrive home and walk my bike to the backyard and let myself into the house.

I'm still not used to coming home before Mom on a regular basis. There is something eerie about arriving to an empty house. Or maybe it's just me. I place my bookbag on the kitchen table and retrieve my list again.

I glance through and figure out what to gather up first. I guess I can grab the cookies from the freezer. I head into the kitchen to start there.

I am doing the finishing touches to my hair. I just keep it simple. Mom tried to do my makeup for me, but I declined. I just put on some lipstick and that is it. I don't like the way I look but oh well. I expect Amber will be beautiful. There's no way I can compare, so why bother? I hear the door knock and Mom and Dad greet Dave. After one last glance at the mirror, I leave.

Andrew is in his chair in the dining room. He's happy and dancing in his chair. Dave is standing there talking to Andrew and holding his hand. I see that and I'm so happy. Dave has really become more natural with Andrew. I smile as I head to him. I give Andrew a hug and a kiss on the top of his head. I have all of the stuff for the prom by the door. With the help of Mom and Dad, we gather all of it and load it up in Dave's car. Once the task is complete, Mom insists on taking a picture. I'm sure I have a stupid smile in the picture. I always do.

After the obligatory picture taking is finished, Dave and I get in his car. I am nervously clasping my hands in my lap. I'm not sure why I'm so nervous. We truly have become very good friends. I've come to find out that Dave understands me better than anyone else. Maybe because prom is the quintessential date night? I don't know. I keep repeating the mantra in my head, "I'm doing this for Amber. I'm doing this for Amber."

Dave isn't talking either. Should I say something? Fill the silence? I've never felt the need to with Dave. I glance over and he seems tense, too. I gather courage. "I am sorry Mom insisted on a picture. I never take good pictures, so I tend to not want things memorialized!" I laugh. "Unless you want a picture of me with a goofy smile!" I purposely scrunch my face to make a ridiculous smile.

Dave quickly glances over and then back to the road. "Nah, I didn't mind. And I'm sure you looked great in the picture. I'll be sure to text your mom to ask for a copy sent so I can show Amber!"

I groan. "No! I don't want that!"

"Why? It's just a picture and it's not like Amber or I would make fun of you. Also, I seriously doubt it'll be as bad as you think it is!"

I quickly glance at him, the tension seems to have relaxed. "So, with all the decorations, food and music, how do you want to get everything set up? I don't really have a good eye. I can put stuff on a table and hang things on a wall, but I'm not sure I can figure out how it'll look. I've always relied on Amber to do those things."

"You can set up the food. I'm not very good at that either. However, Amber can tell me where to hang things for the decorations."

"That's a great idea," I agreed. "Hopefully it won't take too long to get everything all set."

Dave slows down to turn into the parking lot. My butterflies come back. Why am I so nervous? I just hope that there will be no awkward silences.

I attempt to knock on the door, with extreme difficulty. Each of us are laden with bags of food and decorations. As I struggle, a bag of chips falls. "Oh no! Now the chips are going to be tiny and can't be dipped! I'm so stupid!" I pause, and just as Dave was going to say something, I say, "I know, I know. Give myself grace. I am trying, Dave. I guess I'm giving myself opportunities to practice!" I place a couple of bags on the ground and knock on the door successfully. I can hear

Amber as she gets close to the door to open it. She does it without bumping her chair this time. I think, if it were me, I'd bump it every single time.

There are not a lot of differences from when I was here last (two days ago). However, I did notice a new flower arrangement on the table by her bed. "Hi, Amber! Ready to get a party going?" I greet as I enter the room.

Amber is in her chair already. She has on a pretty blue dress and I can tell either her mom or Jenny did her hair. "Oh, Amber! You look beautiful! I love the color of the dress! It fits your blue eyes perfectly! And who did your hair?? It looks amazing! Pfft and look at mine? Just up in a half ponytail!"

"Thank you. As you know, Mom found the dress for me. She and Jenny helped me get ready. They actually just left like 15 minutes ago. They made me promise to take lots of pictures, though."

I groan. "I went through Mom taking a picture of Dave and I. You mean, there will be more? Ugh. I hate pictures!"

Amber laughs and I love hearing it. She is laughing more these days, but still not as often as she used to. "You will have pictures taken and you will love it!"

"Pfft." I start moving the flowers to the end of the table to make room for the food. Dave asks Amber where to hang the decorations. In about twenty minutes the room is all ready, and I open my phone to play music from the Bluetooth speaker. I look from the corner of the room where we placed the empty bags. Amber is in her chair moving the chair to the rhythm of the music and she's smiling. I look and I see Dave trying to dance with her but she keeps "accidentally" running over his toes. I am so glad we could bring the prom to Amber. This is perfect and, to be honest, I think much preferable to the "real" thing. Small, quiet, and with a few of my most favorite people in the world!

I settle in a chair to watch Amber and Dave. As I do, I recall a visit that occurred right after the visit with my family and Dave. I was sitting in a chair by Amber's bed, holding her hand. Amber squeezed my hand. I glanced at her and she took a breath. "I wanted to thank you for bringing *Moth Flight's Vision*. I read it yesterday. So many memories from that one book. I gave the book to Elias yesterday. Maybe he'll become a Warrior Cats fan, too!" Amber smiled at me. "I appreciated your text the other day, also. It was a good reminder to me. It's been hard, and I know it will be hard. But I'm so lucky to have such a good friend. You are my blue skies, Rita. Truly. Oh and, hey, how'd the children's book writing go? Where'd the guinea pigs, or whatever, end up going?" I laughed and let her know they were hamsters. I proceeded to tell her about the book and showed her the pictures I took of it. When I left that day, I hugged her and tears came. Not because of sadness, but joy. Our friendship was intact and still close.

Now, as I sit here watching Amber. It's like nothing has changed, except I know *so* much has. Does that even make sense?

Amber and I are on her bed. Dave and I got her out of the chair, with Amber assisting as much as she could. Dave is sitting next to us by the bed. We are just hanging out and looking at random TikTok videos, joking and laughing. I glance at the clock up on the wall and realize how late it is. I know Dave and I have to go back, but I don't want the night to be over just yet. I give Amber a hug. "I love you!" It's all I can say because the rush of emotions that came in, well I just couldn't put into words.

Amber turns and smiles, "I love you, too." She grabs my hand and squeezes it. "Dad is coming soon with Jenny. Jenny is going to help me get ready for bed and spend the night. We are gonna have some good ol'fashioned sister bonding time!"

"Well, I guess we should gather up some stuff. Want the decorations still up for you and Jenny?"

"Yeah. That'll be fun. I'm sure Jenny will like them and like it even better taking them down!"

I laugh as I sit up from her bed. "Well, I hope Jenny doesn't hate me too much, then!"

I leave the cookies and sweets for Jenny and Amber to have. I gather up the other items. Dave helps, too. In short order, everything is gathered and we are saying our goodbyes when Jenny and her dad come in.

Mr. Ramsey waves at us as Jenny walks in. Jenny exclaims, "Did you guys have fun? Can't wait to see all your pictures!"

"And with that note, I'm gonna say goodbye before the poking fun starts!" I laugh. I give Jenny a goodbye hug, then Dave and I head out.

This has been a really fun night and I'm glad Amber will have her sister to hang out and bond with. She is such a good big sister. I've always been a little jealous that I never really had opportunities like she does to have a "normal" relationship with her siblings. It's nothing I'd ever share with my parents or anyone else, really. But it's there. With my newfound "give myself grace" motto, I have found I can be more honest about my feelings. And not be ashamed of them. It really has been freeing.

We arrive at Dave's car and we place the stuff in the trunk. I get in the passenger seat. "Thanks again for this idea, Dave. You are very creative; I would have never thought of this. It was perfect!"

"Yeah I had fun and I think Amber did too. And you too!" He stops as he starts the car. "I still can't believe Jeremy did what he did. We don't talk much now."

"Yeah. I just have the one class with him. I do find myself glaring at him. I did it today, even!" I give a small laugh, "But, on the other hand, I get it. I see it all the time when we are out with Andrew. People just don't know how to interact around people who are different from them, wheelchairs or otherwise."

"I suppose, but it still is not ok."

"Yeah, I agree."

The rest of the car ride, we played a game we just came up with in the last few weeks. It was "Guess my favorite ___________." If you guessed the other person's favorite item (after three questions), it's your turn to have them guess. It was a stupid little game we came up with one of the many car rides back and forth. However, it has been fun getting to know Dave's favorite candy, song, place, etc.

"Ok, my turn," Dave announces. "Guess my favorite person!"

I laugh. "Can I have more than three questions?"

"Nope. If you win, you need to win legitimately. Otherwise, you'll feel bad and not truly feel like a winner."

"Dangit. You're so right. Curse my sense of competition and fairness! Uhhh, ok, how about: Is the person alive?"

"Yes."

"Ok, so not a historical figure." I pause to think, "Um, is your person on your soccer team?"

"Nope. One more question to go! Be grateful that I didn't count the asking for more questions as one!"

"Whatever. If you had, you would not have felt you won legitimately and *you* would feel bad!"

Dave laughs. "You are so right!"

I regret asking about a specific group. I should have been more vague with my question. "Is the person at your school?"

"Nope. I win!" Dave announces. He starts slowing down to turn onto my street. Wow, the trip seemed a lot shorter than usual. That is crazy.

I start to gather some things. "So are you going to tell me the answer?"

"I don't know. I just might not because I know it will bug you not knowing! It happened with my favorite cookie, remember? You still don't know it!"

"Yeah, and I'm bitter about that!"

Dave pulls in and helps me with the items. We get to the door and I open the door quietly so as to not wake Mom and Dad. We place the bags just inside the door. As I turn to say goodbye to Dave, he motions for me to step outside.

"Yeah?" I say as I step out on the porch and shut the door behind me.

"My favorite person is you, Rita. Thank you for going to the prom with me."

I gasp. It is a surprise, but really not. "I had fun! And, you are one of my two favorite people, I think."

He leans in and gives me a kiss. It was my first one, and it was magical. He steps back and says quietly, "Good night, Rita."

I stay on my doorstep as he pulls out of the driveway, and long after. I am enjoying the breeze and coolness of the night. I don't want to go inside just yet and end this night.

Epilogue

I get out of the car and shut the door. I gather my jacket closer as I briskly walk to the building. It's gotten colder! And glancing at the sky, it looks like it might even snow, it looks like. I really should be better about checking the weather.

As I open the glass door and step into the warmth, I, once again, reflect on how so much has changed in the last 6 months or so!

After graduation, I decided to do two things–drive and go to college. I don't know what made me want to; I suppose it has a lot to do with Amber's accident. I think, down deep, before the accident I didn't think there was anything I had to contribute. So why bother? Not that I'm glad Amber had her accident, but I definitely grew as a person. It forced me to see things in a different light. I have strengths and I should use those strengths.

So, I spent all summer driving and applying to college. And yes, dating Dave. He encouraged me every step of the way. I'm so glad that everything that happened helped me see him in a new light, and him me.

Because I waited so late to apply, I decided to attend our community college for a year. This worked well since Dave is a senior currently. I haven't told him what schools I've applied to next year and he hasn't told me where he has applied to either. We didn't want either of our decisions to influence the other person's decision.

As far as Amber? She is attending the University of Maryland, as planned. She's done well (of course!) this semester. Her parents are in the process of a divorce. So she's home a lot for her siblings' sake. Now that the parents have separated, Amber says things are a whole lot better. Everyone is happier.

Her parents still haven't come back to church. Honestly, I only go at this point because my family goes. I am still questioning a lot, but giving myself grace. I don't have to have the answers.

I finally get to the classroom and sit down in my usual seat. I place my backpack on the ground and retrieve a notebook and pen. I glance outside as I do so. It is still very grey outside.

As my professor starts teaching, though, I'm happy. I know I have a lot yet to learn and grow as a person, but I have blue skies in my life. Blue skies.

Afterword

This book has been loosely modeled after my life growing up. I have a brother with special needs (as well as 2 sisters and another brother) and a best friend that I met in kindergarten. However, my brother does not have cerebral palsy; he had bacterial meningitis at 9 months old in 1981. Thankfully, due to vaccines that they give to children, what happened to Andrew hardly happens now. Also, my best friend did not get in a serious car accident.

However, the thoughts and feelings that Rita had, were thoughts and feelings I remember having as a teenager, both in general and in specific situations.

I was in a creative writing class my senior year, as well. I remember the assignment of describing myself as a color. I had a hard time with the assignment, but I was pleased with my end result. The color I chose was peach.

I hope you enjoyed reading; I have enjoyed writing this book.

September 26, 1995

I asked my best friend to describe me as a color; to give me a few ideas. She thought a little bit and said, "Peach."

Peach? My mind rebelled at the thought. "Why" I asked her, "I mean, peach is so...little girlish."

My friend just smiled and shrugged her shoulders.

But the past few days, I have realized how true her statement is. Peach does characterize me best!

Peach is warm and cheery. I try my best to make people smile and laugh because I hate to see tears. I love to make people happy. Their smiles are reward enough.

Peach can be described as a "shy" color. I mean, in a crowd of other colors, it does not stand out, yet it tends to bring out the other colors more, by complementing them.

Like the fruit itself, I am sensitive and bruise easily. I can be hurt very easily by the words of my friends because I take them seriously, when I probably should not. Although I hurt easily, I also forgive very easily.

Although peach does fit me perfectly, I can't lie. Sometimes, I wish that I were a more exciting color like red or blue or purple. There are times I am unhappy with myself; but I am learning to be pleased with my peachy feelings.

Karin is a special education teacher. She currently lives in Texas with her husband, children and 3 cats, none of which are named Elgato.